ALL THE ROADS THAT LEAD FROM HOME

ALL THE ROADS THAT LEAD FROM HOME

Stories

Anne Leigh Parrish

Press 53
Winston-Salem

Press 53, LLC
PO Box 30314
Winston-Salem, NC 27130

First Edition

Cover art, "Lone Chair," Copyright © 2011 by Lydia Selk

Library of Congress Control Number: 2011914804

Printed on acid-free paper
ISBN 978-1-935708-41-4

To John, Bob, and Lauren,
the three brightest stars in my sky

Grateful acknowledgment is made to the publications where these stories first appeared:

"Surrogate" won first place in *The Pinch's* 2008 Literary Award, and appeared in their Spring 2009 issue

"An Undiscovered Country" received an Honorable Mention in the 2009 Arthur Edelstein Prize for Short Fiction, and was published in the Writing Site's Featured Writer Series in July 2010

"Loss of Balance" was named as a Top Twenty-Five Finalist in *Glimmer Train's* Summer 2007 Fiction Open and was later published in the October/November 2007 issue of *Eclectica Magazine*

"For The Taking" was a Finalist in the Salt Flats Annual 2007 Emerging Writer Fiction Contest. The story was published in the May/June 2007 issue of *River Walk Journal*, and later included in the anthology *Late-Nite River Lights*, published by EditRed Books

"Pinny and The Fat Girl" appeared in Issue 38 of *Storyglossia*

"All The Roads That Lead From Home" was awarded First Place in *American Short Fiction's* 2007 contest, and appeared in their Summer/Fall 2008 issue

"An Imaginary Life" appeared in Issue 31 of *Storyglossia*

"Snow Angels" was published in the June 2010 issue of *PANK Magazine*

"The Comforts of Home" was the first piece of original short fiction published by *Chamber 4 Magazine* in November 2010, and also appeared on the website for their new literary venue, *C4* in February 2011

"The Fall" appeared in Issue 3 of *Prime Number magazine*

"Our Love Could Light The World" appeared in the March 2011 issue of *Bluestem*

SURROGATE

The statue was really a lawn ornament, a crude Madonna, between three and four feet tall. They'd gone to the garage sale to find a crib, but when Maggie saw the statue, she just had to have it. What pulled her in was how the mother's head, arm, and cradled child made one smooth arc, to represent the essential—the eternal—flow of life.

She wanted it where the dining room table was, in front of a bay window that looked out on a strip of dead grass, so Donny moved the table into the hall, and then to get around it you had to squeeze, not easy to do with a growing stomach.

There would be more room for everything if the previous owner hadn't split the house in half. What used to be a good-sized living room and study were now a separate apartment, and Maggie and Donny had bought the house for that very reason. Donny thought the extra rent would help with a baby on the way, and in a couple of years, when they needed more room, they would break through the wall and add about nine hundred square feet to their living space.

Then the baby was no longer on the way but dead, and removed with an injection of something to bring on labor. It was a girl, as Maggie had wanted, with a tiny face so absurdly human it made her weep. For two days she lay in her hospital bed tormented by memories of her mother who abandoned her at age five, her father whose ashes she'd scattered just last summer into the blue water of Lake Cayuga north of Dunston, her doctor saying she'd conceive again in no time, and a social worker who said grief is a process, a slow hum forward.

Maggie didn't want to go forward. She wanted to stay where she was and let the world leave her behind.

But the world dragged her along. The crib and changing table they'd ordered arrived in flat boxes Donny propped against the wall by their front door. Maggie stubbed her toe on them several times before her body learned to sway to one side when passing by.

The caretaker of the cemetery called to ask when she wanted to come and choose a headstone. She refused to choose a headstone, so Donny and his mother, who'd come down from Buffalo in a snow storm, did. Donny's mother rented a motel room for two weeks and appeared every day to make casseroles, clean, and fold laundry. She complained about the placement of the furniture—*Jesus, Donny, you got the whole place upside down here*—said the table should go back by the window, and the statue out in the yard where it belonged. *Don't you dare touch it*, Maggie whispered so hard that spit flew from the corner of her mouth. Donny's mother brought her a cup of tea, *here, take this, don't be silly, I went through it myself after Donny's father died*, and said that sooner or later Maggie would come to see that life belonged to the living.

In February, four months to the day of the miscarriage, a bird flew into the glass of the bay window and dropped dead into the bushes. Donny went to remove it. Maggie watched. Her hand dropped to the statue. She ran her fingers along the cold, smooth stone. She met a notch, a flaw, she hadn't noticed before.

In the spring their tenant, who'd brought cookies and flowers when she'd heard their sad news, moved out. She left a smear of pink nail polish in the bathtub, five empty pizza boxes stacked on the kitchen counter, and took away in return a picture of a little girl with a swan which had hung above the sink.

Donny hired cleaners, then painters to brighten the walls to their original, antiseptic white. He replaced the leaky faucet, installed a new light fixture in the bedroom ceiling, switched the sofa with the love seat to make the living room look larger, and even set some bright, plastic dishes out on the kitchen table with cheerful cloth napkins. Maggie thought he was nuts. Donny was patient. He talked about strategic marketing, creating a positive impression. She didn't care if they found a new tenant or not. Again, Donny was patient. Empty space like that was a waste when it didn't generate something, he said.

He placed an ad in both the local and student newspapers. Several people came to look it over, then didn't return. After the apartment had been empty all summer Donny stopped talking about lost money, and said they should start the remodeling project they'd first planned on.

"Oh, Donny," said Maggie.

"Why not?" He'd downed a few beers and was sweaty and red-faced. He was celebrating. Sales figures for the month had been posted, and once again he'd sold more cars than anyone else. Maggie didn't know how he did it. All that charm and energy, day after day. Even after the baby died, he barely slowed down.

She sat across from him at the table. Behind him and facing her the statue stood, still as ever. The kitchen window let in the smell of someone's barbeque. Donny ran his thick hand through his hair and then watched her. She hated it when he did that. She helped herself to a small spoonful of last night's macaroni and cheese.

"I don't see the point, that's all," she said.

"Look. I know it's a little sooner than we planned, but I think we can swing it. We're making decent money."

Now probably wasn't the time to mention that she was probably going to get fired. She was a cashier in a grocery store by the university. She couldn't stand all the nerdy college students, not to mention the ones from God knows where, who could barely speak English. Just yesterday she'd raised her voice to one, and her boss, who long ago stopped being sympathetic about the miscarriage, said her attitude sucked.

"Drop it," she said.

After dinner Donny wrote up a new ad, making the apartment sound much nicer than it really was. *Territorial view. Newer appliances. Large parking space.*

Two weeks later a young woman came to see it. She wore sky blue eye shadow, torn jeans, and smelled like beer.

"You take kids?" she asked Donny.

"It's only got one bedroom," said Maggie.

"Doesn't matter. She can share with me, 'less of course I have company. Then the sofa's fine for her."

Donny turned red. The woman didn't seem to notice. She'd gone into the bathroom, and was opening and closing the cabinet door.

She returned to the dining room. "Place come furnished, then?" she asked.

"Yes," said Maggie.

"When can you move in?" asked Donny. His color was still high.

"Monday. That's when I got to be out of my other place."

"We'd like a reference from your current landlord, if you don't mind," said Maggie.

"Oh, no, you don't. He'd just give you a bunch of bull."

"Even so, I really would prefer—"

"Listen. The guy's a major turd. How come you think I'm getting out?"

The woman removed five one-hundred-dollar bills from her pocket and gave it to Donny.

"You give me a receipt for that later," she said. "Oh, and I'm Jo."

"Jo," said Maggie.

"Short for Joellen."

Later, Donny counted the money again. Maggie lay down and stared at the ceiling above their narrow bed.

"I like a tenant who pays cash," Donny said.

"Good for you."

Donny folded the money, put it in an envelope, then licked the envelope and sealed it.

"That's disgusting," said Maggie.

"What?"

"You. That sound you made."

"What sound?"

"With your tongue."

Donny stared at her. Sometimes, when she was lying down, he lay down with her, and before too long his hands would go inside her shirt. She hoped he had no such notion at the moment. He put the envelope in the inside pocket of his jacket, which lay across the bed at Maggie's feet.

"Donny," she said.

"What?"

"Nothing."

"It'll be okay." He meant the noise a child would make, after what had happened.

The little girl, Shauna, made no noise at all. It was her mother who stomped, clattered, banged doors, and yelled. Sometime she yelled at Shauna. *Pick that up! Put that down! Go to bed!* Maggie watched them come and go, Shauna always walking behind, looking at the ground. She was probably around five. She went to day care in the morning, and didn't come home again until six or seven in the evening. Sometimes a man brought her home and stayed until Jo's car appeared in the driveway. One time he didn't. Maggie watched his rusty Chevrolet blow out smoke as it went off down the street.

Maggie pressed her ear hard to her bathroom wall. It was the one place where she could hear most clearly what went on next door. She heard nothing. A few minutes later she stood in a scratchy evergreen bush and peered through the living room window into Shauna's apartment. Clothes were scattered across the floor. A beer can lay on its side. A liquor bottle was visible under the couch.

Shauna trotted from the bedroom to the hall in a pair of hot pink pajamas. She dragged a chair from the dining room into the kitchen, climbed onto it, opened a cabinet, and took down a box of cookies. Then, with the box in one hand, she dragged the chair back to the table.

Maggie's firm knock was answered after a long silence by Shauna saying, "Go away!"

"That's not very nice. Besides, I know you're in there."

"I'm not allowed to talk to strangers."

"I'm not a stranger. I'm your landlady."

"We don't have a landlady!"

"Of course you do, and that's me. I'm also your next-door neighbor." Maggie stood on tiptoes and tried to see down through the half-moon glass at the top of the door.

The silence resumed, though by the time Maggie realized she could use her duplicate key to get in, Shauna had opened the door. She looked up at Maggie with cold brown eyes. She was African-American, Maggie realized, seeing her up close for the first time.

"That man that was here, what's his name?" Maggie asked.

"Uncle Frank."

"I see. Well, Uncle Frank shouldn't have left you alone."

"I don't care."

"Well, I do. You come next door with me for a little while."

"You got a TV?"

"Oh, yes. A nice TV. Come on, I'll show you."

"You got Teletubbies?"

"What's that?"

"My favorite show."

Once inside Maggie's apartment, Shauna went straight for the statue. They were about the same height. Shauna then turned to Maggie and said, "It doesn't have any eyes. How come you don't color it some?"

"Well, because it's not—"

"You got crayons?"

"No, I'm afraid I don't. Why don't you come and watch TV, instead?"

Shauna didn't budge. Maggie wondered what she had around to bribe her with. There was some Halloween candy that was almost a year old, but that didn't seem like a good idea.

"Or maybe you'd like to look at my jewelry box. I used to love looking at my mother's jewelry when I was a little girl," said Maggie.

Jo's pickup truck rumbled up the driveway. Shauna ran to Maggie's front window and slapped her little hand on the glass. Jo got out with a bag of groceries in her arms. When she saw Shauna, she yelled, "What the hell you doing over there, girl?"

Maggie opened her front door, and leaned on the jamb with folded arms. "Staying with me. Your friend left her alone."

"Really? When?"

"I don't know. Half an hour ago, maybe."

"Huh. Well, he's a right SOB, that's for sure." Jo closed the door of her truck with her foot. Shauna trotted out to her.

"Mommy, you're late!"

"I know, baby. I'd have got here a lot sooner if that jerk at the store had taken my damn check. Know what he made me do? Use the cash machine. Only it was out of cash, if you can believe that, so I had to find another one."

"I'm hungry!"

"Well I've got something for you in here, if you can wait one minute. Now, get the mail for me."

Shauna trotted down the walk to the twin boxes in front. "Nothing!" she called back.

"Nothing from your dad?"

"Nope."

"Shit! Fucking deadbeat." She turned to Maggie. "Oh, and thanks for watching her. I'd return the favor if you had one of your own, but seeing as you don't, guess I'm off the hook!"

She grinned, went inside, and Shauna skipped in after her. Maggie stood a few minutes longer in the silence they'd left, then went to her couch, and sat with her head in her hands.

"So, like this guy, this retarded guy comes through my line, right? And he's touching the damn conveyer belt and saying, 'It just goes around and around and around,' and his keeper, aide, whatever, is looking at a magazine. God! Drove me nuts," said Sally.

The overhead light in the lunch room made the dark line beneath her eyes even darker. Maggie slipped off her shoes. She had ten more minutes of break. She rubbed her neck, and stretched her shoulders. Her body always felt so cramped and sore, as if she were hiding in a box.

"What's got you so bummed?" asked Sally.

"Nothing," said Maggie.

"Don't give me that shit. You're always bummed."

Sally was two years younger than Maggie, twenty-eight, and had four children, two from two different men she hadn't married, and a set of twins by a man who'd been married to someone else at the time she got pregnant. The kids stayed with Sally's mother most of the time, even when Sally wasn't working. Sally's new boyfriend didn't like children and couldn't stand to be around them. Maggie thought he'd get Sally pregnant one of these days, and then she'd have one more little bundle to unload on Grandma. It just wasn't right, all those healthy babies cast off like puppies to an animal shelter. All Maggie had wanted was one.

Maggie's red sweater was tight and itchy. With her white *Customer Service* smock she looked like a candy cane. She'd worn it because her boss, Mr. Dominian, had said to look more cheerful.

Making an effort then, are you? Donny had asked that morning as they got ready to go. She said nothing, only pulled her hair brush through and through again.

Maggie helped herself to a cigarette from Sally's pack on the table and lit it with Sally's lighter.

Sally yawned.

"Jesus. What a night. Kyle's teething and I was up with him three times," she said.

Maggie didn't reply.

Sally looked at the clock on the wall, and then at her watch. She lit a cigarette for herself, and slid the pack into the pocket of her smock. "So, you guys going to try to get pregnant again?"

Maggie exhaled a plume of smoke.

"You still want to, don't you?"

Maggie shrugged.

"*Can* you?"

"So I've been told."

"So, what's the problem?"

Maggie considered the red ember of her cigarette.

Sally leaned in towards her. "Is it Donny?"

Maggie shook her head.

"Then it's you. You're off sex. Is that it?"

Maggie crushed her cigarette into a yellow, ceramic tray that bore the store's name in loopy red letters. Ever since losing the baby she couldn't stand for Donny to touch her. At first they both thought it would be temporary, but it wasn't. She said she wasn't ready, and he offered to use a condom, but she refused. In the last year they'd made love maybe four or five times.

"Can't you just shut your eyes and pretend he's someone else? Some hunk?" Sally asked.

Donny was actually very good-looking.

"Get plastered, first. Rent a dirty movie. Wear sexy underwear."

"Oh, shut up."

"You have to do something. He'll dump you, if you don't. Men don't like dry spells."

Maggie knew Sally was right, that Donny wouldn't put up with it forever. But she couldn't make herself feel something she'd forgotten how to feel, something that had become alien, so weird she found it stupid even to try.

The ice cream left a thin brown trail that ran from Shauna's lower lip, down her chin, onto the little hand clutching the cone, and then into her lap. Maggie passed her a piece of tissue from the box on the seat between them.

Sliding by the car windows were trees aflame with autumn color, and the air—the whole world—seemed to glow.

Maggie was babysitting. It was Saturday. Jo had called that morning to say she had a chance to take an extra shift from four to eleven. "Best time for tips," she said. Maggie held back. She didn't want to seem overeager, so she said she needed to check with Donny to see if he'd made plans. He had. To play golf with guys from the dealership. Maggie called back to say sitting would be fine, just this once.

"Cool," said Jo.

Maggie picked up the phone again.

"Did you change your mind?" Jo asked.

"No, of course not. Listen. Does Shauna have something to keep her busy? Some toys, maybe?"

Jo laughed. "I used to be like that before her. Wondering how to keep us both from going nuts. Sure, I'll send her over with stuff to do."

Maggie's refrigerator had sour milk and a six-pack of beer. For lunch she'd finished the Chinese take-out Donny had brought home the night before.

"I don't know. She's not a picky eater," Jo said when Maggie called a third time.

"But I haven't been to the store yet."

"I'll make her a sandwich, then, okay? It's not that big a deal."

They were at Maggie's door promptly at 3:30. Jo had fresh highlights in her hair, polish on her nails, and cherry gloss on her lips. Work, my eye, Maggie thought. A date was more like it.

Shauna sat down at the table and ate the sandwich she'd brought with her. Her jaw worked slowly, and she hummed as she went along. Then she took out some paper and crayons from her Barbie backpack, spread them out, and started to draw.

Maggie asked her if wanted some tea. Shauna stared at her, then shook her head. Of course she didn't want tea, Maggie thought. What kid drinks tea?

She went in the kitchen and put the kettle on to boil. She glanced at Shauna every now and then while she waited. All of a sudden, she wasn't there. Just as Maggie turned off the stove, something shattered. In the bay window Shauna stood holding a crayon. Maggie pushed passed her and looked at the chalky fragments of statue on the floor. She knelt, and lifted the broken face with the red, sloppy leer Shauna had given it. Beside it the trunk of the mother was now a gray, empty space.

It was hollow! No wonder it tipped so easily! Month after month it had stood there taking up room, being a nuisance, and filled with nothing at all.

On all fours Maggie gathered the pieces together, then she sat and looked at them.

"You gonna spank me?" asked Shauna.

"No, of course not. Just help me sweep this up."

When they finished, Maggie said they were going for a drive. The note she left Donny said, "I've gone to fall into Fall." He was always saying how she'd fallen in on herself, like an old barn in a field, though she doubted he'd see the connection. He might not even notice that the statue was gone, either. These days his eyes were either always down, or aimed at some distant point beyond her and the walls around them.

Shauna rolled down her window and threw her cone onto the road.

"What are you doing?" Maggie asked.

"I couldn't eat any more."

"Well, you shouldn't have done that. It's littering!"

"You don't have a trash bag in here."

"No, but—"

"I got to go to the bathroom."

At the next exit Maggie turned into a small park she had visited as a child. The willow trees bent towards the water, and the wind covered the surface of the lake with white arcs. The air had turned cooler with both the hour and the season, and she wished she had a coat.

The bathroom was a low, concrete building with hundreds of small spiders suspended in webs across the ceiling. Shauna was scared of them, so Maggie said she'd stand guard and swat any that tried to come near. Finally Shauna used the toilet, then refused to wash her hands. Maggie let it go. A car pulled in next to hers and the passenger got out. She laughed and staggered towards the bathroom. The driver, a man, looked just as drunk. His head was thrown back and he laughed too, his shoulders heaving up and down.

The laughter stopped when Shauna opened her door into his. The man's head pulled up straight and turned in Maggie's direction. His eyes were bright and cold, even though he was still smiling. He rolled down his window and said, "Tell your kid to watch out."

"It was an accident, she didn't mean—"

"Then she's a clumsy little fuck."

Shauna looked the man right in the eye. "Bite me," she said, then hopped into the front seat, and pulled the door closed behind her. Maggie started the engine and pressed the button that locked all four doors at once. Once she'd backed up, she hit the gas fast enough to make the tires chirp. Then she laughed so much it was hard to drive.

"Are you gonna tell my mom I said that?" asked Shauna.

"I think I should."

"She says it all the time, but I'm not supposed to."

"Well, that makes sense."

"Why do grown-ups get to say bad things and kids don't?"

A deer bounded lightly across the curving road and melted into the bushes. Maggie slowed to see if there were others. There weren't.

"We have different rules," said Maggie.

"Why?"

"Because we have to do things kids don't have to."

"Like what?"

"I don't know. Be responsible. Make hard choices."

"Oh."

"Of course, some choices get made for you, and then it's like being a kid again."

"Why?"

"Because you don't have a say in what happens."

Shauna watched the trees and hummed. Then she stopped. "Can we get some leaves? My mom likes leaves. She puts them in a big book, and then we look at them sometimes."

Maggie pulled over where the shoulder widened. They walked a little way into the woods. *Swoosh, swoosh* went the dead grass below.

Shauna trotted ahead. Maggie stood, enchanted by the spread of red and yellow at her feet. That death should cause such beauty made no sense until you realized what it made way for—the next round of burgeon and loss.

She looked up. Shauna was gone. Maggie called her name, then louder, until she screamed *Shauna!! SHAU-NA!!* From behind the trunk of an oak tree many yards ahead Shauna's head appeared, then her small body.

"You come right here, right now!" Maggie shouted. Shauna obeyed, her eyes on the ground. In her hands were a cluster of red leaves.

"I'm sorry," she said.

"You scared me."

"I was playing Hide-and-Seek."

Maggie's hand found Shauna's spongy hair. "You can't play if the other person doesn't know you're playing."

"Can we play now?" Shauna's eyes were bright, even in the deep shadows of dusk.

"No, honey, it's getting late."

At the car Maggie took the leaves Shauna had gathered, removed the last tissues of Kleenex, and put them in the empty box. It was dark enough then to use her headlights. They'd been gone more than four hours. The long side of the lake was the one they were making down now, and it would be another hour and a half to home. She could turn around, go back and save time, but she wanted to keep moving forward.

Shauna sat with the box of leaves in her lap. Soon her chin dropped to her chest, and her eyes closed. Even tough little girls get sleepy, thought Maggie. And Shauna was tough. She'd never let anything slow her down for long, and she'd give as good as she got.

Have I?

A waxing gibbous moon rose in the purple sky. Another day or two and it would be full.

How like the sky the night she learned she was pregnant. Lying in bed then she'd loved the near fullness of the moon, and the slight fullness in her. Donny laughed and said you couldn't be a little bit pregnant, so how could you be a little bit full? But fullness did come in degrees, just like emptiness.

She'd been as empty as a person could be. And then she'd just gotten used to it, and didn't see the point of changing. Donny accused her of letting it work for her in some way, of taking some benefit from the deep bitterness within.

You're too lazy to go on living, he'd said. How she'd resented that! She lay in bed a whole day afterwards, and refused to unlock the bedroom door.

It's not just you, Maggie. I lost the baby, too! It was the first time he'd ever yelled at her. Then he left for hours, and took himself on a long drive, just as she was doing then.

Sometimes it was better to move than to stay still.

It goes around and around and around.

In the inky, starlit dark, Maggie followed the curve. The lower lake was darkest as she rounded in to Dunston. The lights came up in bits, and then more and more, like an idea taking shape.

It's time. Life over death now.

The windows of her apartment were bright. Maggie turned off the headlights, and then the engine. She got out, went around the car, and opened the door where Shauna was sleeping hard.

Donny came down the steps. "Where the hell have you been?" he said. He smelled of sweat and beer. His hair was spiked in a way she knew, from him running fingers through over and over.

"Driving around the lake. I didn't think I'd be gone so long."

"Your note didn't say anything about driving around the goddamned lake."

"I'm sorry."

He was so close she felt the heat of his body. On winter nights, before the baby ever happened, he could keep her warm all by himself.

"I figured you got pissed off and left," he said.

"Why?"

"The statue. The pieces were in the trash, so I assumed you broke it."

"It was Shauna."

Shauna opened her eyes. "Mommy?"

"No, honey. It's Maggie, remember? We're home."

Shauna looked at Donny. Donny stared back. "Come on, now. Let's get you inside," he said.

Maggie undid the seatbelt and Donny slid his hands beneath Shauna. She seemed small and light in his arms.

She accepted being put down on their bed, and then having a blanket pulled over her. Maggie sat with her, rubbed her hand, remembered a song then didn't sing it.

Shauna turned her head, and soon, as she breathed softly, they stood and watched her in the moonlight.

"I'm sorry about today," said Maggie, in a whisper.

"It's okay."

"Didn't mean to scare you."

"I know."

Shauna shifted, then was still.

"Donny?"

"Yeah?"

"You know what I've been thinking?"

"What?"

She didn't have to say a thing. It was there in his eyes, even before she touched him, that he already knew.

An Undiscovered Country

My mother had a way of dropping by at a bad time, a habit that got worse after she died. There I'd be trying to set the table, wash the dishes, or get Eric to bed, and in she'd waltz and ask when I was going to get a life. This, from a ghost, was not easy to take.

Forget being scared. Forget being shocked. That's for people who think there's a hard line between the living and the dead. You see, I've always known my mother was the haunting kind.

That said, I have to admit the first time totally freaked me out. Not just by seeing her all of a sudden, but by what I was feeling right before—like an epileptic who smells something weird then seizes up, though I'm not an epileptic, only someone who thinks too much sometimes—and it had been an overthinking sort of day, so I'd taken a shower to relax. My face itched—I have a nasty birthmark below my right eye I call Blobbo and it was tingling. As if it were coming to life—like your foot when it's been asleep. I turned off the water, tugged back the curtain, and there she was handing me a towel.

JESUS CHRIST! I shrieked.

Don't be silly, Darling, I look nothing like him.

She was always witty. Always the card.

I knew I'd lost my mind. She assured me I hadn't. I asked if she were real. She said, *As real as you need me to be.*

I hate to say it, but her tone was almost flirty. Enticing. This wasn't my mother. My mother never cared if she pleased or wounded. This was some awful figment—yet her face was the same. Those thick eyebrows and hooked nose, the small, pursed, pouting mouth. And her perfume, Chanel Number Five, only . . . fresher. As if newly sprayed. That gave me the creeps worse than anything.

I dried off, put on my bathrobe—one she'd gotten me two birthdays before—and asked the obvious questions. *Why are you here? What are you made of? What's it like, where you are?*

Look, this is as much a surprise to me as it is to you, was all she said.

From then on she appeared at will, sometimes only in a dream, or a random memory, but more often than not as a fairly solid being who'd picked up tea drinking somewhere—not in this world—and always had a steaming cup at her elbow.

This morning she's here again at my table doing a crossword puzzle. I'm not happy to see her. I guess I can't get used to having breakfast with a dead woman. I plop the laundry basket down on the table next to her, hoping it'll make her vanish.

"How industrious you are," she says.

"You sound surprised."

"Not at all. I just wish you'd show your good side more often."

I give her my good cheek.

"Oh, for heaven's sake!"

My son, Eric, is on the floor, lining up his screwdrivers. Eric has Asperger's, a mild form of autism. He doesn't connect the way other people do. Can't pick up the social cues (as in Okay, you've said this nine times, you can stop now); can't read expressions (Yes, that look of irritation on my face is real, so please don't bother me), that sort of thing. Which basically puts him in his own world. A world with a population of one. Along with the things he picks apart—toasters, old computers, my hair dryer. Once he dismantled a brand new vacuum cleaner. There were pieces of it scattered all over the living room floor, and he put it back together perfectly.

"Why do you look at him like that?" my mother asked.

"Like what?"

"Like a dog who's just had a boo-boo on the rug."

"I don't know what you're talking about."

"I think you do."

She used to say I wasn't affectionate enough with Eric, that I kept too much distance between us. I'd like to see *her* try to get close to a kid with emotional problems. Maybe then she'd get off my case.

I fold the laundry. Something of my mother's has made its way into my basket, a lace camisole I don't ever remember seeing. I toss it in the trash. My mother doesn't notice. Her mind's on her puzzle. The crease between her eyebrows deepens. Her lips pucker, as if she's about to deliver a kiss.

"Help me with this, won't you?" she says.

"You know I'm no good at those."

"Nine letter word: 'Go beyond, in a spiritual sense, perhaps.'"

"Transcend."

"See?"

She's been dropping these stupid hints for days now. I'm suppose to *transcend* my life. How, I'd like to know. I have a job I hate and can't afford to quit. I work at an auto parts store in a windowless, wood-paneled office that smells of stale Mexican food from the drive-in next door.

I also have a kid who'll never fit in. Eric's day care lady says he'd probably do fine next fall in kindergarten, but I'm not sure. He can get plenty pissed plenty fast. Throws things. Pulls his hair. She says he's frustrated because he can't communicate very well. She says everyone will make an extra effort, but how long will that last once they see what he's really like? Then I'll get pulled aside for friendly chats and told I have to try harder at home, as if this is all my fault, somehow.

As the morning light rises, the blue ceramic tile backsplash in the kitchen deepens to sapphire. It really pops against the white cabinets and countertops. I chose it. My mother probably thinks it's overdone—garish, she might say, and I knew that when it went in, and yes, I took pleasure in that. You see, this is her house. I inherited it. I had no idea she'd left it to me. The lawyer told me she hadn't, in fact, because she didn't have a will. But that, a mutual fund and an insurance policy that together added up to about twenty grand came to me as her only surviving relative. Just like that. Poof! I moved right out of my apartment. Sold off my shitty furniture, and started replacing some of hers. There was a lot of going through drawers, donating clothes, throwing out endless magazines and coupons she never used. In the pantry were about fifteen boxes of cookies, mostly mint Oreos and Nilla Wafers. She ate those by the handful in front of the television, talking to the screen, calling the people on it names. Sometimes she laughed, or made a joke. And sometimes I'd laugh with her. We weren't anything like good friends, but we got along okay. Enough for me to feel bad she was gone. I even felt rotten once or twice, and when it really sucked I just kept going, moving down the chore list. I tossed out her knick knacks. Ceramic owls, if you can believe that. I wasn't allowed to touch them when I was little. *You better be careful, Sheryl Lynn, or one of those owls might just come to life and bite you! Then you'll have two marks to deal with!* The sound of them shattering in the trash can was beautiful. The roses were next. Dug them out myself. A bank of white and yellow Queen Margarets she tended as if they were the baby Jesus. They drove her crazy. About every other year they'd spot up, get these brown stains on the petals. She consulted someone at the university, some botanist. I don't know if he told her anything helpful. She put special mulch around the base, sprayed them, watered them only at certain times of day. Once I found her crying over them. It was crazy.

"'Something you carry for a long time.' Six letters," she says.

"Grudge."

"Right you are!" She fills in the boxes with a smile and a jaunty toss of her head. I can't take it.

"Look. Just tell me what you want and then vaporize. Okay?" I say.

"Are you trying to get rid of me?"

"Oh, for God's sake! Of course I'm trying to get rid of you! You're a fucking ghost!"

"Such language." She clicks her tongue. "Well if you *must* know, I'm here to see something through. And to make you see through something." She smiles to herself.

"Yeah? Like what?" I ask.

She wags her finger at me to say she's explained enough.

Yesterday, my boss asked why I was so crabby. I said I hadn't been sleeping. He sat in the chair across from my desk and said, "Sherry, what you need is a little romance." His bald head turned pink with the effort it took to say this. "I mean it. You're young. You're pretty. No, you're beautiful. Go make some man happy. Better yet, let him make you happy."

He wants to set me up with his son, Derek. Derek is twenty-eight, six years younger than I am, and hung like a horse. I know this because he got drunk one night after work and displayed his equipment to me back by the spark plugs. Derek's just a fun-loving guy who can't keep it in his pants. He's screwed every woman that ever worked here except me. Ed, I suppose, thinks I'd get him to settle down. Ed thinks I'm highly capable because I have a kid with a disability and come to work made up like a starlet. Little does he know how horrible I'd look otherwise.

"But seriously, what's really going on?" Ed leaned forward, his gut flopping over his gray polyester pants.

"My mother's driving me nuts."

"Your mother's dead, Sherry."

"I know that, Ed."

"She got killed in that wreck on I-80 last spring."

"Yup."

"I was with you at the funeral." His voice took on a soothing, keep-her-calm tone. He leaned back and checked his watch. Derek sauntered by my open door, saw us, then backed up. "Hey, Dad. Sher. What's up?"

"Your father thinks I'm nuts," I said.

"He's right." He grinned.

"He doesn't believe that my dead mother comes by every day and tells me how to live my life."

He stopped grinning. He scratched his head. "Huh. Weird shit happens sometimes. You just gotta go with it, I guess."

Ed waited to see if I'd say anything else. When I didn't, he said, "Okay, folks, we're on the clock here." He gave me a worried glance on his way out.

On Sunday my mother fades a little. She's there, but harder to see. "What's up?" I ask.

"I'm moving on, that's all. You didn't expect me to stay forever, did you?"

Eric's father said the same thing just about the time he started fading out, too.

I never signed on for this, he announced when we found out Eric was autistic.

And I did?

Hey. You could have gotten rid of it.

'Him,' not 'it.'

The day he moved out, Eric sat on the floor and said, *go-bye, go-bye, go-bye,* for about four hours straight. Now, when my mother mentions leaving, Eric looks at her long and hard, with a lot more interest than he usually shows anyone.

"I thought you said he couldn't see you," I say.

"What? Oh, well, maybe he can. Who knows?"

I stroke Blobbo. It's soft and smooth. Touching my face in the dark you'd never know it was there. *I can't even feel it,* Eric's father once said. To be honest, Blobbo didn't seem to bother him much. He confessed that he thought it made me vulnerable, needy for the attention I probably didn't get. I translated that to mean he thought I was easy. And I suppose I was.

Since him, there have been two other losers who felt sorry for me and came home. Joe-Joe, the guy who fixes my car, and Alan, a guy at the hardware store. I gave them what they needed. Maybe they were grateful, or sated for a while—*meaning full up, replete, needing nothing more.*

Christ, now I sound just like her. My mother was a high school language arts teacher. She hated it, thought her students were a bunch of morons. She was so tough on them that one took a magic marker once and wrote "Hard-ass bitch" on the windshield of her car. I can just imagine how she was in class. Her voice pleasant, and her words like ice. *You should really try to be more careful with your makeup, Sheryl Lynn. That foundation may not suit you as well as you think.* I'd started wearing it in junior high. I'd reached a point of despising Blobbo. Years of laser treatments had faded it only a little, and I couldn't stand the sight of myself in the mirror. If I were home without make-up on, and someone called to say they were dropping by, I'd run to the bathroom and start slathering it on. Only my closest friends ever saw me without it. They were kind, I guess. One said Blobbo looked like a map of something, a country no one had yet discovered, that I alone had the secret to. Her name was Evelyn. She killed herself our senior year in high school over some boy. When my mother heard that she said, *Well, that's not something you'll ever do, is it?* Meaning I'd never be able to get that deeply involved with anyone, because of my looks.

Sometimes I think she was just trying to train me not to expect anything but disappointment. Other times I think she took out on me things she didn't like about her own life. Not being able to find another man after my father booked out made the list. Not having much money did, too. What she hated most was having to pretend to be happy. My mother didn't drink, but one night she got drunk. She'd been to a party at another teacher's house, and really poured it down. She was driven home, seen to the front door. She always worried about what people thought, so for her to let go like that was really weird. She found me in the living room, wondering where the hell she was. Out of the blue she said, *Some day you'll be glad you were born like that, mark my words. This world is so full of phonies!* In the morning she had no memory of saying anything to me, let alone of getting home from the party.

Eric lines up his tools, now that he is finished putting my clock radio back together.

"All fixed!" he says, with a bounce. This is the true Eric, underneath it all. Proud as pie about what his amazing little hands can do.

My mother taps her pencil on the table. "'The real McCoy.' Seven letters."

"Genuine," I say.

"One smart girl, you are."

Eric's up on his feet, his coveralls twisted. He wants a hug. He doesn't want them very often. I hug him. He smells like sour milk and sugar. He hugs me back, and pats my face. He does that sometimes. He thinks Blobbo's a riot. Once, he traced it with a Sharpie. Took me days to scrub it off.

We pull apart. My mother's gone. So's the crossword puzzle, her pencil, the tea, and that scent of Chanel. I walk room to room, and even look in the closets, but I know she's disappeared for good. Don't ask me how, I just do.

The next morning I'm late getting up. Weird dreams— none about her, about my high school days. I was picking a place to sit in the cafeteria. The boy I liked had to be on my good side, which was tricky to arrange because that chair was taken. Then it became a game of musical chairs, everyone walking around in a circle until the music stopped, and no matter what, I always got the wrong damn chair. When I finally did, the boy wouldn't turn the other way, wouldn't let me see *his* whole face. I felt totally ripped off by that, and I woke up feeling flushed and cold at the same time.

Eric doesn't want to go to day care, which makes everything a struggle. He sits at the table, swinging his legs, not eating his cereal. I give up, haul him into the car, and take him to the day care lady's house. She stares at me. I don't know why. Eric's in clean clothes, his hair is brushed, I've packed his lunch. I even remember his beloved animal crackers, though she wouldn't know about that.

At work everyone's clustered by the sales counter. Janice, the cashier, is saying Ed's a sitting duck. She says there have been robberies in the neighborhood, and they might be the next target, especially after six when Ed takes over from Janice and he's all alone. As I draw near three faces turn my way. Conversation stops. They stare.

"Whoa, Sher," says Derek.

"Whoa, yourself."

I knew I shouldn't have worn this sweater. It's a little clingy, and Derek being Derek can't resist. But what's Ed's problem? And Janice's?

"What's this I hear about robberies?" I ask.

"It happens. Goes with the territory," says Ed. He's trying not to look at me.

"I say protect the territory," says Derek.

"We've got an alarm system," says Ed.

"That's for the store. Doesn't protect *you*," says Janice.

Ed reaches below the counter. He's got a baseball bat down there! Derek steps back. Janice laughs.

"How long have you had that?" Derek asks.

"Since this morning. I listen to the news, too, you know." Ed chokes up his hands and cocks his hips. "Come on, buddy. What you see is what you get!"

We all laugh. But then they turn to me again, so I make for my office. I sit. On my desk is another stack of invoices. I have to make sure they all add up. So, that's what I do, number by number.

On break I hit the Ladies Room, which is just the common bathroom for all of us, and Janice's job to keep clean which she does for shit, and there I am, in the tiny mirror over the sink, totally makeup-free. Crap! How the hell did I manage that? No wonder everyone's freaking out! Blobbo's having itself a field day! For a moment I think I'm going to puke. Slowly my stomach settles. My face is burning. I tap cold water on my temples. I could bail out, rush home, and return intact, but what's the point? My makeup only does so much. Blobbo's still visible, a faint shadow, no matter what. Who have I been kidding?

"You okay in there?" Janice calls through the door.

"Be right out." I guess I've been holed up in here for a while. I can't hide forever. I return to my office, past Janice, who watches me go.

Back at my desk my right hand flies to my rescue, even though I'm beyond rescuing. I used to sit like this, chin to palm, and pretend to be deep in thought. Trouble is, I'm right-handed, so when I had to write something, I had to show myself. I tried writing with my left hand. Ambidextrous sort of thing, only it didn't work. *Sherry's handwriting has become increasingly poor this quarter*, one teacher wrote home.

Stop it, my mother said, crumpling that note. *Just stop it!*

I force myself to concentrate. The invoices add up. Ed's spends a lot, and makes a little more than he spends. That's the way it's supposed to be, I guess, if you call yourself a going concern.

At lunch we brown-bag it in the break room. No one talks, and no one looks at me funny, so maybe one of them said something to the rest, but then I don't think so, because they all just seem lost in their own heads.

Then Derek says, "Dad, that's my old bat, isn't it? From Little League."

"Yup," says Ed. Derek, a Little Leaguer? Don't exactly see that.

"Can't believe you still have it," Derek says.

"I wouldn't throw something like that away."

"Dad used to coach me," Derek tells me and Janice. "He was pretty tough."

"Too tough, sometimes," says Ed.

"Nah, you were fine."

"You quit because of me. Because I was such a bastard about your swing."

Derek looks thoughtful. Clearly, he'd forgotten that episode.

And that's when I remember my last conversation with my mother, the day she died, as she got into her car to drive to the mall, minutes before a semi jumped the median and hit her head on. She was talking about my life again, saying I'd turned into a recluse, afraid to take a chance. She said, *You don't have enough confidence to open up, because*—I'd rolled my eyes, turned away, and didn't give her the chance to finish. If I had, I'm pretty sure she'd have said something like *because I've been so critical.* She'd been reflecting on things a little more those last few weeks. As if she were trying to come to terms, put things in order somehow, or at least make amends. Maybe she had a premonition that she wasn't going to be around much longer, I don't know. I'll never know.

"She's gone," I say, suddenly.

Derek puts his plastic cup on the table. Janice looks up from her magazine.

"Who's gone, Sher?" asks Ed.

"My mom."

"We know, hon. We know."

"No, I mean she's really, *really* gone."

They expect me to cry, I think, because they're all there around me, hands on shoulders, murmuring tones of comfort.

I don't cry. I don't laugh. I only turn to the window which shows a slice of blue sky so lovely I can't speak. When I turn back I realize I've given them my bad side. But it doesn't matter at all because I'm no worse than they are. I'm no worse than anyone, and I never was. That's for sure.

LOSS OF BALANCE

The woman in green talks again about her boy, Joey. Her face bears all the pain he's put her through, the broken promises, the stolen money, the calls from the police. Joey can't stop shooting drugs into his arm, so he's in rehab again. Only on Thursday he gets out, and this woman, whose name you can't remember, is sure the cycle will start all over.

She doesn't know what to do with Joey, and you don't know what to do with your father. Your father is not a drug addict, only an old man who likes to give his money away. Joey has a problem with self-control, your father has a problem with self-control, so you, the woman in green, and five others who bear responsibility for a wayward soul meet today with Dr. Schiff in a church basement—the best he could arrange after hearing that his office had flooded overnight.

You don't want to be here, but your husband insisted. He says it's time to get at the root. When your father's retirement home called last month to say he'd written them a bad check, you paid the bill, then went into a bit of a tailspin, it's true. *What's pissing you off goes a lot deeper than money,* your husband said. Maybe yes, maybe no. The point is, you recovered. You always do.

Dr. Schiff—Leonard—moves on to Edmund. Edmund's wife is an alcoholic. She hides vodka everywhere, including the toilet tank where Edmund discovered two bottles when the plumber came to fix a leak. Edmund told the plumber the bottles were his.

"Did anything bother you about that?" asks Leonard.

Edmund seems to consider the empty space above Leonard's head. Finally he says, "Yeah. The look on his face."

"And what look was that?"

"Like he was sorry for me, like he knew I was lying."

Edmund's eyes are troublesome. One is blue, the other brown. Leonard's eyes are like dark honey. Their deep grief says how much the world has had its way with him, how much he's given up against his will.

Edmund says nothing. Leonard lets the silence continue. People stare at their own hands. Someone coughs. Your mind wanders. What are you going to make for dinner, you wonder. Is your husband going to be home before you? And what about the yard work you've been putting off— all those shrubs to be dug up and replaced with something more attractive?

"Ralph," says Leonard. "How's it going with Lisa?"

Ralph's daughter shoplifts. She's thirteen, and has been in and out of juvenile detention.

"Fine," says Ralph.

"Just fine?"

"Well, I had to tell the police she's getting counseling."

"I see."

"But she's not, is she?" says Miranda, whose sister steals, too, but only from family.

"No," says Ralph.

"Because she doesn't think she has a problem." Miranda's eyes burn with bitterness. Miranda's sister ran up her credit card in Vegas for over ten thousand dollars, then begged for a plane ticket home.

"Right," says Ralph.

"She probably thinks *you're* the one with the problem."

Ralph nods, his big eyes sad, like a spaniel's. He has big ears, from which tufts of hair reach out. His shoulders are huge, but his feet are small. You've never seen a man with such small feet, smaller even than Leonard's, which sit primly in their shiny brown wingtips.

The church basement is cold, and hard morning light breaks through high windows. The gray carpet is stained with coffee, and you imagine Styrofoam cups in the hands of pious people, deciding how best to raise money for that new steeple. You are not a churchgoer. You're not an atheist, exactly, but the idea of organized religion sits poorly with you. Your father was once a Quaker, a leaning he inherited from his mother, a woman you didn't know and of whom he said little, except that she never raised her voice. You cannot imagine this petite, quiet woman. You're neither petite, nor quiet, facts your father seems to regret when he looks at you.

"Darlene," Leonard says. "Why don't you tell us how it's going?"

You shift on your metal chair. Your pantyhose make a rasping sound as you cross your legs. You can't think of anything to say.

"Have there been any more incidents?" Leonard asks, urging you with those anguished eyes.

"Well, yes. He wrote another check."

"A big one?"

"Two thousand dollars."

Ralph whistles. "That's not chump change," he says.

"Who'd he give it to?" asks the woman in green.

"An old student of his. Guy got a Ph.D, then some teaching job that fell through."

How can you ask me why, Dar? Because I know those clowns who denied him tenure. No job, and stuck at home now with a sick baby. Didn't know that, did you, about the sick baby?

A sick baby would be easier to handle than your father.

After the bounced check to the retirement home, he took cash advances on credit cards whose monthly payments he can't meet. It's less important to stay current with them, since there's nothing they can attach if he doesn't, but staying current with the retirement home is key. If he falls too far behind he'll be asked to leave, and his only option then will be a Medicare facility, which wouldn't have the wide green lawns, nice artwork, and afternoon teas he has now. *I don't care about any of that, Dar. I'd be happy in just a little room. As long as it's clean. And has the* Golf Channel. *I've come to enjoy the* Golf Channel *quite a bit.*

"What kind of loser asks an old man for money?" asks Miranda.

"He didn't ask. My father offered."

"I should get his number." This is from Janice, the group's most hardcore sufferer. Her husband sleeps with any woman who will have him, and apparently many will. He always returns, and she always takes him back.

"What does he say when you ask him to stop?" the woman in green wants to know.

"Nothing."

Because you never asked him to stop. You can't even bring yourself to remind him that he owes you money for the retirement home bill.

"Sounds like my daughter," says Ralph. "Just looks away and pretends not to hear."

Nods of sympathy all around.

Janice's cell phone rings. She grabs it from her battered vinyl handbag, stares at the caller's number, then silences it. No one asks if it's her husband. Everyone knows it is. He calls with an excuse, a lie, a story, to say he's working late. All eyes are on her now. Everyone feels her pain. As she returns the phone to her bag you see that the laces of her athletic shoes are mismatched. One is silver, the other white.

Leonard concludes by asking everyone to reflect on the limited ability to control another person. Living with destructive behavior can turn us into control freaks, he says. To regain your balance, you'll have to find a way to accept what you can and cannot change.

This is where you're way ahead. You've known forever that there's no changing your father. Who he is was determined years before you were even born.

Your mother always blamed him on the war. Your father was an ordinary person with an extraordinary ability to recognize complex patterns. This was not a skill he knew he possessed before a military analyst discovered it. How the discovery was made you're not exactly sure. Some aptitude test, probably, which quickly eliminated the possibility of active combat and moved him right into code-breaking. After the war, rather than make a full-time career in military intelligence, he became a professor of history. His time was divided between known events and secret ones. How he reconciled these two worlds you don't know, except by what he said and what he didn't. He was open about his life in the university, winning grants, beating out colleagues for promotion, but on the military life he continued to lead when called upon he was, by necessity, absolutely silent.

The balance he struck didn't work for your mother. She needed all of him, not part, and left after twenty years of marriage.

She was soon replaced with a second wife who had no interest at all in your father's secret world. You were replaced with a stepdaughter—Leslie. You grew up, got married, lived your life. You had regular contact with your father, cordial and impersonal correspondence, brief well-managed visits. You always wanted more. There was never enough real interest in who you were, as if your father could have been sitting across from anyone, instead of his only child. How that hurt! How hard to keep that hurt secret—your own secret—your own dual life.

Not long ago the second wife died. Your father paid you another visit. Although it had only been about a year since you'd seen him, you thought how much older he'd become, how frail. For a moment your heart went out to him, the lonely widower. You prepared a nice dinner, and got a bottle of Johnny Walker Red, his favorite. He was grateful. He enjoyed himself. He mentioned the sale of the house he and his second wife had long occupied. You said you were glad, because he'd have plenty now to meet the retirement home's steep entry fee.

Oh, I'll have to scramble a bit for that, he said. *I let Leslie have it all.*

You fell silent. It's possible you even made a face, because when you father looked at you he said, *She needs it, Dar. She's had such a hard time.*

The hard time, you soon learned, consisted of not being able to find a job, not being able to make the rent on her small apartment every month, not being able to find a good man to spend time with, and so on. Then your father added that he wouldn't need his car at the retirement home and would give that to Leslie, too, since her car was so old and undependable.

He went to bed early, not long after you cleared the table. You sat in the living room alone, drinking your own gift of scotch, and drafted the letter you'd write the next day to Leslie about responsibility, trying harder to get a job, not taking money from your father, who had reached the time in his life when he must survive on a fixed income.

Her return letter arrived quickly enough to make you certain that she felt terribly guilty. She didn't feel guilty. She wrote:

It was weird to hear from you after all these years. You don't exactly stay in touch. Your father used to say he wished you'd pick up the phone or drop him a line once in a while. I hope you're not mad I said so. I'm very concerned for your father's welfare, as you know. I've made every effort to keep him company these last few months, and I don't mind telling you that your poor father is very grateful to me. The time I spend with him has made it hard to develop my pet sitting business. Your father is very supportive of my career. It gives him pleasure to extend his support and thanks to me. I know you understand that it would be unkind of me not to accept it.

You remember Leslie as a child when you were still one, too, and the visits to your father's new home on Sundays, the one day the divorce agreement allowed. Leslie's mother insisted on eating in the formal dining room, an ugly box with deep red wallpaper and dark, heavy furniture. Conversation centered on your father, his students, the papers he was grading. And then it always came, that moment when Leslie wouldn't eat her vegetables. Your father made her sit at table staring at her cold plate, while you stayed tensely in the living room. You wonder how she has forgiven him, and think maybe she hasn't, that wanting money lies behind her kindness. You're proven right, because with the house gone, and the car in her hands, she's nowhere to be found.

You skip the next meeting of the group. Things have gotten crazy at work. You're facilitating the acquisition of a large electronics company by an even larger discount chain. The dreary time you spend negotiating the buyout ratio makes you regret majoring in economics. You would have preferred to study English Literature, but your father discouraged you on the grounds that he wanted you to make a good living, and not struggle for money the way he always had to.

Several days later a social worker from the retirement home tells you long distance that your father fell in his room and needed to be hospitalized. His condition isn't grave, but she thinks now would be a wise time for a visit.

During the three-hour drive northward from Virginia, you consider the information you received about the incident in question. Your father was standing on a chair which he'd brought into his closet. There was something he wanted on the top shelf, what, you don't know. You don't know what things he brought with him from the old house. You don't even know what his room looks like. As to the fall itself, it was assumed that fluid in the inner ear was to blame for the loss of balance, also the medications he took to control blood pressure, and quantity of scotch consumed against the advice of his doctors.

The hospital hall is quiet and the rubber soles of your shoes squeak on the flecked vinyl floor. The noise slows as you near his room. You're afraid to enter, afraid of your own thudding heart.

His eyes open at the light touch of your hand.

Dar, is that really you? Did you really come all this way?

With a little tease in your voice you say, *Come on now, don't sound so surprised.* Then you look for evidence of Leslie, some gift she might have left, a bouquet of flowers or a box of his beloved chocolate cream. There's nothing.

You take a chair and draw it to the bed. You mention the weather there in Pennsylvania, and remark that your spring at home is several weeks ahead. How silly you sound, because any fool knows that spring travels from south to north.

The radiator bangs, then hisses. The ugly beige curtains don't quite close, allowing a column of glare to fall across the floor.

The nurse comes to take your father's temperature. She takes his blood pressure, too. She refills the pitcher of water, slides the thermometer from his lips, reads it, and drops it in the pocket of her bright, floral-print smock. Then she's gone. You wish she were still there, occupying space between you and your father.

Guess they told you what your dopey 'ole father did. Sailed right off that damn chair. The bruise on his cheek is florid and difficult to look at. There were no major injuries, otherwise. He's being kept for observation only, for an assessment of his mental state, and to determine if he's fit to return to independent living.

Suddenly his face tenses, and his eyes focus on you hard. You're reminded of a picture taken years before, a candid shot by a student wanting to capture your father in mid-lecture. The expression is the same, fierce, intent, totally absorbed.

Did I ever tell you about Stu Drake? he asks you.

You hear that Stu was another Illinois grad whose straight teeth and high grades put him in the cockpit by the summer of '42. Stu wrote often about training paratroopers, the wide billow of the silk growing smaller as they dropped away.

So, that's what your father thought of as he fell. About dead soldiers, their chutes becoming shrouds.

Your words, not his. The drive has made you punchy. And the call from your husband on your cell phone as you reached town, his voice full of remorse about last night's disagreement which you can't at the moment remember.

Did I ever tell you how I wanted to be a pilot? Failed the physical. Know why? Your father taps his crooked front teeth. *Wouldn't fit inside an oxygen mask. Probably saved my damn life.* His voice becomes as thin as the late afternoon light. *I was lucky. Luck is a kind of responsibility, and I didn't know what to do with it.*

He wants something to drink, something alcoholic, which he's not allowed. You consider buying him a bottle, hiding it in your large, messy handbag, and sharing it as the night comes on. You won't, though, because he's still talking and needs your audience even more than he needs the alcohol.

She hated me for what I did. I suppose she told you all about that, though, didn't she? Sometimes I feel like picking up the phone and trying to set the record straight, but what's the use? Your father has forgotten that your mother's been dead for ten years. *She thought I was arrogant, do you know that? She accused me of thinking that ordinary people were too stupid to be trusted with the knowledge I had, but that wasn't it at all. I couldn't talk about my work because I took an oath of secrecy. An oath is supposed to mean something.*

Information has become declassified and television shows about the war years, specifically the code-breaking efforts on the part of the United States and Great Britain have aired, yet your father keeps quiet.

He's grown tired, and closes his eyes. In a few minutes he's sound asleep. It's unnerving to sit there, with him so still and peaceful. You feel as if death could enter at any moment without your knowing. But he's not close to dying. He won't die for another four years, by which time you've given him a very late-arriving grandson whose creation took faith and artificial means.

Later you stretch across the orange bedspread in your motel room and think of your father trying to make up for being lucky, for not talking, for wanting Leslie to eat her vegetables, but not for you, never for you. Maybe in his eyes you just weren't weak enough.

How well you've turned out, Dar. You've got such character. Don't need a thing from anyone. You're one independent gal.

His words, not yours, whenever the conversation failed, as it always did, because you didn't want him to call. Didn't want to tumble into something you didn't control, where the weight was all on his side.

In the morning you find you've slept in your clothes, and the bed is as rumpled as you, but only on your half. You call your husband. He's glad you did. He wants to know how your father is. *Out of it, really out of it,* you say.

You say you'll be home tomorrow, and remember to say that you love him.

I love you, too, Dar.

Your father is awake, and has had his breakfast. Egg has spilled on his front. He's fretful, and his bent hands pluck at the bed sheets.

I don't know if I can go on helping my friends, Dar. I think I've run through all my money.

You nod.

I hate letting them down, but I don't know what else to do.

You're at a loss now, in the face of this candor, this worry. Your father never showed worry before. Only steely calm, even when his second wife berated him, or when Leslie said she hated him, or when you accused him of arrogance that day on campus.

You make people into puppets! Sitting there in the dark, pulling strings! You'd learned that he had put in a good word at a college you'd applied to, just as a way of helping things along. You didn't want help. You had faith in your own merits, or at least you argued that you did. In truth you had no faith at all.

For a moment your waving arms and loud voice seemed to throw him off balance. His face opened, then closed right away because someone walked by and called his name, a colleague with a briefcase and expensive shoes. As your father called back you walked off, perhaps not having the will to try to get his attention a second time.

You didn't go to the college he talked to. You went somewhere else, far away out west. The desert air was good for you. You put down roots in the dry ground, yet you returned, not to your home town, but further south. Why did you come back East at all?

"Can you help me, Dar?" Your father's voice is quiet. He doesn't look at you. "I think I may need help."

"You mean pay another bill?" This would be as easy as

the last, because you and your husband are frugal, even cheap, and you've got a lot put by. The balance in your money market account alone is over sixty thousand dollars.

"No, no, I couldn't take a penny from you. Just help me manage what I've got. I can't seem to keep track of it these days," he says.

You agree to take a look at his checkbook and see if you can make sense of it.

He directs you to his rooms, his "cottage," he calls it, at the retirement home. The receptionist in the main hall opens the door for you, but doesn't leave you the key. The front room is larger than you expected, with a sliding glass door. Outside the door is a small concrete slab meant to serve as a patio. There's a single folding chair there, and an empty glass someone overlooked. You lift the glass and smell it. You bring it inside and rinse it in the tiny stainless-steel kitchen sink.

The bedroom is much smaller. Cardboard boxes line one wall, stacked three high. The dresser is low, one you remember from childhood. A bright red drop of nail polish, like plastic blood, remains in the corner where you spilled it over thirty years before. The checkbook is there, in the top right-hand drawer, just as your father specified. You toss it on the carefully made single bed. The closet is almost too small to get the chair into, but you manage. On the shelf are boxes with letters inside. None are from you, because you never wrote. There are sweaters, shoes, a curled-up belt, a hat your father must have held onto from the Fifties, the last time anyone wore such a thing. There is also a framed photograph of you. You're not smiling. The background color is too brightly blue, and you remember it as your class picture from the fifth or sixth grade. Unlike everything else on that shelf, it's been dusted, kept clean.

Was he getting it down, or putting it back? Or just taking a moment to look at it, wipe it off, then return it to the dark? There are no other photographs visible in the tiny apartment, or in any of the drawers you go through, even those in the kitchen, only yours.

You take the glass you just rinsed and fill it with a little scotch from the bottle by the toaster. On the small sofa you drink some, and then drink some more. The lake can't be seen from where you sit, but it's there for sure, long and deep, only a few miles away. On its shore there's a park where you went in summers before your parents split up. You fill a blue plastic bucket with pebbly sand and take it to where they lie on wide, striped towels. *What a pretty bucket*, you father says, rising up to see better. Then, *I have a secret to tell you! The secret is I love you! Now off you go, find me some more sand for your bucket.*

Years after the bucket is lost you eat a TV dinner in your father's dark apartment. There's a game on the black and white set, the antenna off kilter, the picture in and out.

Who scored? he calls.

Pittsburgh, you're happy to say, knowing the teams at last.

He stands in the low kitchen doorway, a can of beer in his hand. He says he's getting married again soon. You nod. *Mom told me,* you say.

The final quarter is underway, Pittsburgh reaches Miami's 10-yard line, and still in the doorway your father says, *I want you to know that I won't have any more children. You're the only child I have, the only one I want to have.*

Years later you call up to say you just got married. A silence falls on the line. In the background there's a game playing, and you have to wonder if it's football. *I wish you'd told me, Dar. I would have liked to give you away.*

You finish your drink. Something within you shifts, then drops like a single flake of snow. You put the glass down, and sit a little longer in the quiet of your father's empty house.

You find the checkbook in the bedroom. Inside bears your father's neat, square hand. You take it along to look at later, and realize how very glad you are you made the trip.

For the Taking

Angie needed a drink and had already waited ten minutes for Fran to offer her one. Finally she went into the kitchen, found a glass, and returned to the living room. She joined Fran on the soft leather couch and helped herself to the whiskey from the crystal bottle on the coffee table.

The funeral had been long. A lot of people Angie didn't know gave voice to her father's good deeds, *I remember when he taught Bess to play her first scale,* and *He guided Collin through his first recital.* Fran was the last to speak. She cried as she described their seven lovely years together—*a second marriage for us both but even better than the first*—then closed with *your music is silent now, my love, though for you my ear remains keen.*

To Angie, it was a big bore. She'd given up on her father years before and was only there to get something for her trouble, something she could take away and hang onto.

"Find out about insurance," Kevin had said as Angie boarded the bus to Ann Arbor. "An old guy like that, he'd have insurance." He didn't, though. He didn't have a will, either.

"Because he wasn't planning to die," said Fran, when

Angie asked why not. "Don't you think he'd have put his affairs in order, otherwise?"

Angie sipped her drink. Her father was only sixty-two. He'd been a piano teacher. Angie's mother had been one of his students. Their marriage was four months older than Angie, a last-minute arrangement, she was always told. Angie was five when her mother ran off with another man, and she remembered nothing of it, though her father said she'd been right there, watching the car drive away. What Angie did remember was her mother's absence, the sudden silence in the house, and then a postcard from Montana saying, *I made a mistake.* Her mother didn't write again, she didn't come home, and went on living with her mistake, Angie hoped, until word came of her death from pneumonia in an Arizona hospital three years later.

"There are a few photo albums you can have, and some costume jewelry of your mother's, although I don't know why he kept it, under the circumstances. Oh, and you can take the ashtrays. You know how he loved those," said Fran.

And the bars he lifted them from, with Angie on the lookout, those many nights when staying home was no comfort at all.

In the beginning they were turned away. *What are you thinking, trying to bring a child in here?* In time they were allowed to stay. And stay they did, through the lunch crowd, the after-lunch crowd, the happy-hour crowd, smoke and laughter taking them towards night. *Everything I ever learned, I learned in a bar,* Angie had told Kevin more than once.

What she learned was how to use silence and wide eyes to get pretzels and soda, sometimes a sandwich, sometimes a sweater or a pair of shoes that no longer fit the bartender's son or daughter. People gave you what they thought you needed easily enough. The trick was getting what you wanted.

"What about that old piano?" Angie asked Fran.

"The one in storage? Goodness, I'd forgotten all about it."

Angie's father discovered it in the basement of a church where he'd woken up after walking the streets and screaming at the violet sky. Angie had spent the same night alone in their drafty house, with only the television's gray-blue face for company. Later at the church she held her father's sweaty hand, thought of how hungry she was, and looked at the piano. Tiny painted roses decorated the closed keyboard lid. The finish was dull and scratched, something her father pointed out while he haggled with the Father.

You've a keen eye, the Father said. *I can see you're a man of taste. If I weren't a good Christian I'd drive a harder bargain, but the truth is that this room's to be converted, and we've no more need of it.*

Then the Father asking her, *Can you see yourself here, playing those fine, round notes all up to Heaven?* His hand in her hair, on her neck, then under her shirt because her father was gone then, off to the bank for the money, and the Father said he'd give her breakfast because it looked like she could use it, but all he did was tug her forward *why don't you and I just sit here a bit, on this nice, fine bench? What a shame it is to let it go.*

"Well, it's yours for the taking. I suppose you'll want to sell it," said Fran.

Angie didn't know what the piano was worth. Maybe a thousand dollars. That would be a lovely windfall. She could get that leather coat she'd had her eye on, and that silver-and-turquoise bracelet she and Kevin saw at the mall. The rest she could bank for that rainy day that always came along so fast. Kevin, though, would want to put it up his nose. His cocaine habit used up all the money his father gave him. There was more money to be had, but his father had become difficult and cut off his allowance.

"Good plan. Better to sell it here, though, don't you

think?" Angie told Fran. That way Kevin wouldn't have to know a thing. *Listen, Babe, things didn't work out so well. That Fran, she's got things tied up tight. Must be how my old man wanted it, leaving it all to her. Figures, doesn't it?*

"Suit yourself, only I'm leaving first thing in the morning," said Fran.

"Really, why?"

She spoke of a brother out in Santa Barbara and needing a change of scene. It occurred to Angie that she could do with a few more days away from Kevin. They'd come to that hard point between lust and love and spent more and more time on their bare mattress, a mattress she'd like some sheets for to cover the brown stains of her period, and the yellow stains of her sweat.

"I've got enough for one night at the motel, but after that I don't know," said Angie and glanced at Fran, who stared firmly into space.

"I can stake you to a second night."

"Oh, you're sweet! But don't you think it would be easier if I just stayed here? After you're gone, I mean. Don't like to be underfoot."

Fran turned her leaky eyes on her. "I'm sorry, honey, you can't."

Angie had visited last year with Boomer, Kevin's predecessor. When they left Fran found herself missing a silk scarf, a pair of gold earrings, and a fountain pen she'd won in a church raffle. Angie sometimes wore the earrings and scarf. The pen she'd never used. When her father called to report the loss, Angie blamed Boomer. She said he was a recovering heroin addict (he wasn't), and that he'd spent time in jail (he hadn't done that, either). Her father believed her. Obviously Fran didn't. Boomer, who knew nothing of the theft or the phone call, moved out several weeks later when he realized Angie had been helping herself to his wallet.

Fran offered to ship the piano down. Ann Arbor to Dunston was a pricey distance, a fact Fran regretted with a lift of one eyebrow. Angie wasn't moved. There'd be no distance if Fran had stayed put. When Angie struck out on her own at seventeen, with no desire to finish high school, Fran pulled up stakes and dragged her father back to her hometown so they could float on the sale of her late husband's grocery store chain, forget the past, and begin again.

Angie wrote her new address on the back of a museum flyer Fran had on the coffee table by the whiskey. *The French Impressionists. February 4th - March 31st. Gauguin, Renoir, Cezanne.* Angie couldn't imagine her father going to see that kind of nonsense, but then with Fran her father always thought he was better than he was.

"Well, then. I'll call a mover. They'll let you know when to expect it," said Fran, and drained off her glass of whiskey. She stood and tugged the jacket of her stylish black suit into place. Angie got up, too. She towered over Fran. Angie was five foot ten, skinny as a boy, with size-ten feet. She'd stuck out at the funeral with her torn jeans and red linen jacket. She looked down at the white roots running through Fran's dyed black hair and kissed her hard, right on the top of her head. Outside, the heels of her cowboy boots banged on the wide brick steps. Above her the sky was a tender blue, the yellow clouds a dream.

Fuck, she thought. It would have to be a beautiful day.

The piano was an upright, not a grand, and because a ramp had been built for a handicapped tenant some years before, the movers were able to get it inside Angie's apartment without loading it onto a dolly.

Angie shoved it around the coffee table, which she realized later could have been pushed aside, to the wall by the kitchen. The wheels gouged the wood.

"Cool," said Kevin when he came in. Then, "Look what those morons did to the floor."

"Yeah."

"Better not lose my damage deposit."

He smelled of cigarette smoke, which meant he'd been with Ramon again. Ramon was where Kevin got his coke. If he had any now, it would have been on loan, because Kevin's father was still being a jerk. Angie had met Ramon only once. He was so short she could have put her chin on his head. He worked as a car mechanic and promised to get Kevin hired on to do oil changes. Of course nothing had come of it.

Kevin went to the kitchen and made himself a peanut-butter-and-jelly sandwich. Marta, his German shepherd, clacked across the floor and sat politely in front of him. He offered Marta some sandwich, then pulled it back just as she opened her mouth to take it. After the fourth time, Angie said, "Stop being such a mean fuck and give her some." His blow sent her sideways into the kitchen counter. The blood tasted like metal and made her suddenly remember falling on the school playground. Kevin stared at her. He was still chewing. The hand he'd hit her with had opened from its hardened fist and was poised in mid-air, fingers bent, like an old man's.

On the street, without her coat, she shivered. Her lip went on bleeding. She could feel it swelling. The Chinese restaurant smelled of hot grease as she passed. Bits of paper lifted in a gust of wind, swirled, then floated back to the sidewalk. At the corner a homeless woman sat on the steps of the church, her garbage bag below. She wore new track shoes with silver laces.

They looked at each other. "Somebody got you good," the woman said to Angie. "Somebody with good aim." Angie stood with folded arms. Her lip throbbed. Behind a square glass pane on the wall by the door the message

"I AM THE LIFE EVER AFTER" stood in white letters, advertising the sermon that coming Sunday. "You go on in, clean yourself up," the woman said. She drank from a tall plastic coffee cup, then looked at her wristwatch. Not homeless, Angie realized. Just sitting there.

"What you doing, girl?" Angie asked.

"Name's Yolanda. Waiting on a guy. Coming to get a donation."

"Of what?"

"What you think? Clothes. Food."

"In a bag. You put it in a bag."

"You got something better?"

Angie went up the stairs. Inside was dark and smelled of dust and wood. The daylight leaked through the stained-glass window. The ladies' room down the hall had a scent of bleach. Angie examined her lip in the small mirror over one of the two porcelain sinks. She felt her teeth. None were loose. On her way out a bulletin board with squares of bright paper caught her attention: *Babysitting, call Clair. Moving? call Jerome. Yardwork. Home Health Aide. Used van for sale. Wanted, upright piano for Church Basement/Nursery School.*

Angie took the long way home, down the street towards the record store and dry cleaners, then past the park where the children were warmly dressed. She kept walking until she was too cold to walk anymore, and then she went home.

Kevin watched her across the candlelit table. The sky had given in to snow and the power had gone out. Angie wore long underwear beneath a cotton skirt. On top she was naked but for a jean vest of Kevin's she'd grabbed in the bedroom. They'd had sex for hours. He'd dug inside her until she was as dry as dust.

"God, you have great tits," he said.

"For a skinny girl."

"For anyone."

Kevin leaned back in his chair, his arms folded across his bare chest. Angie admired Kevin's arms, his shoulders, too. Sometimes she pressed her teeth there, and sucked up the salt on his skin.

"Know what I think?" asked Kevin. "I think you're the kind of girl who can take a whole lot of a guy."

"You'd know."

"Maybe you can take some more."

"Maybe."

She sipped icy vodka from the coffee cup. In four days her lip had healed a lot.

She'd been hit by men before. Not by Boomer, whose real name was Brad. The nickname had come from his mother, because he'd been such a loud baby. He wasn't loud when Angie met him. He never once raised his voice to her, except when he found out about the money she'd taken from his wallet. He called her a cunt, which hurt more than she thought it would. Before Brad there was Toby, a bicycle messenger. He didn't hit her, though she'd hit him for cheating on her with their downstairs neighbor. Before Toby was Pat, and Pat had blackened her eye when she wouldn't get him another bottle of beer.

Kevin looked at the piano. He asked her again about selling it because now Ramon was pressing him for the two thousand he owed. Kevin's father was out. The last time Kevin called his father said, *It's time to face facts. All the money in the world's no use to you. And when are you going to get rid of that slut?* Angie didn't think that was the word his father would have used, and that Kevin had chosen it for effect.

"I'll get on it," she said. She thought of the ad she'd seen, and of the piano returning to a church, going back where it came from, like ashes to ashes and dust to dust.

She laughed softly, then with a harder edge. Kevin went on watching her with his blue marble eyes.

Ramon sat at the far end. Angie waited for Noreen to get him, but it wasn't Noreen's station and Noreen knew it, so she let him sit.

He had the fidgets. One thick tattooed arm jiggled on the bar, one leather-clad boot danced on the bar rail.

"Hey," said Angie, and put a clean square napkin down in front of him. "Where's Kev?"

"Thought you could tell me." He pushed his sunglasses to the top of his head.

"He said he had a job interview."

"Not likely," said Ramon.

"No, probably not."

He asked for a scotch and soda. She mixed it and brought it to him. He stirred it with the red plastic stick she'd dropped in.

"When you see him last?" he asked, looking at her tits. She saw herself in his eyes. The blonde dye she put in three months before had slid down and left a wide cut of black. Her pink tank top and the cold in the bar brought her nipples up like two ripe olives. Kevin's words, not hers. Angie had never eaten an olive in her life.

"This morning. Why?" she asked.

"He owes me money."

She leaned over the bar. "You'll get it."

"I better."

He drank his drink and she pulled back, towel over one shoulder, held by what he was about to say. And when he did she didn't have to agree. That's how it worked when you were there for the taking. Nothing had to be said.

"Ramon says he'll drop it to a grand and call it even," said Kevin. Angie went on washing the dishes. In the dark window over the sink he stood reflected, hands on hips. He was a handsome man, with a fine square jaw, not at all like Ramon. Ramon's nose was broken, his skin was pocked, and his nails were filthy, but he trembled when he held her, even once cried out her name, and then talked of bad dreams, bad things remembered.

"That's good," she said, looking at the tall image behind her.

"I just don't get it, though. He was so hot for me to pay up."

"I know."

"He even went looking for me, down where you work."

"I was there."

He shifted his long, lean weight. She had to move fast, before he added it up. She turned off the water and rubbed her wet fingers on her worn-out jeans. The blood rushed in her ears, down her back, all the way to the soles of her feet. She'd crossed more than half the distance between them by the time he caught her by the shoulders. They made it all the way into the bedroom with her mouth pressed into his.

Kevin had a plan. He knew two things: where Ramon kept his money, and where he kept his coke. "Cash in a coffee can, right there on the shelf. And the coke's sitting loose in an old box of laundry soap." Ramon also had a gun which he kept in his bedside table drawer, and another one in the kitchen, inside an empty fruit bowl on the top of the refrigerator.

"Sounds risky," said Angie.

"Only if I get busted, so I don't lift the coke. The cops won't ask about the money if they find it on me."

"Still."

"Come on, he's got at least a couple of grand. Plenty to go somewhere new. By the ocean, maybe."

"He'll know you took it."

"That's just it. There's this girl he used to live with, this Marcy something, and she's bad news, let me tell you. She comes in and helps herself to everything. He'll have to figure she took it. She's always after him for something. Major sleazeball. No surprise there, given the kind he likes."

He dropped off and she was left to take one deep breath after another until she finally gave in to sleep.

In the rain she made her way down the block. The street was brown with dirt. Her skin was brown, too, and always had been. The big secret. Her father not her father. Her mother a woman who loved brown men so much she got knocked up by one, then left her husband for another.

The driver of a car honked because she was walking in the street. "Fuck you!" she yelled.

She loved him anyway. The drunk who took her into bars.

The rain bent her face down, and when it lifted up there was Yolanda coming around the corner with a wastebasket she must have emptied into the dumpster. Yolanda said, "I remember you." She had cornrows for hair, violet half moons for fingernails.

"You looking for a piano?" said Angie.

"Not me, the Father."

Angie didn't like the sharp stare she was being given.

"All right, then. Don't be standing around in the wet," Yolanda said.

She followed Angie inside and set the wastebasket on the floor. She went down a hall and knocked on one of the doors, then leaned her head inside. She closed the door and called back to Angie, "He be right out."

Yolanda went down another hall while Angie waited. The quiet was broken by the quick tapping of a radiator that slowed, stopped, and resumed like a sick heart not ready to quit.

He came out the door Yolanda had opened a moment before, a short, round man wearing black pants, a priest's collar, and a ratty gray sweater.

"I'm Father Mulvaney," he said and extended his hand. Angie didn't take it. "I understand you have a piano."

"I can let you have it for fifteen hundred," she said.

He nodded, rubbed his hands together, and stared into space just beyond her shoulder, as if he'd forgotten what he was going to say.

"Hm. Now, what kind of instrument is it?" he asked.

"Old and banged up."

"An upright?"

"Uh, huh."

"Out of tune, I suppose?"

"Probably."

"Why are you getting rid of it?"

"What do you think?" Angie had put a few paces between her and the Father by then. He took her in with one long hard look.

"I think you could use a hot cup of tea and a sandwich. I'm just about to have one, myself."

Angie hadn't eaten breakfast that morning because she'd forgotten to get to the store the evening before. Sometimes she ate at work, if her boss left early. Last night he didn't, and she'd had two bags of M&M's for dinner.

"Nothing fancy. Just ham and cheese," he said.

His office was small and full of books and papers. The radiator's paint peeled gray flakes that showed a darker gray underneath. She sat in the chair opposite his, separated by an old wooden desk. On a smaller table were a plate with several sandwiches, a teapot, and a number of cups, most of them chipped. Angie looked at the amount of food, wondering.

"Yolanda always finds a guest or two for me at the last minute. Saves the kitchen trouble by just having something made in advance," said the Father.

"You must feed a lot of people," she said.

"The mission down the street had to close its doors, and the economy hasn't picked up as much as we'd hoped."

Angie finished her sandwich quickly and the Father offered her another. She took it, but refused any tea.

She looked through the window into the courtyard where a man swept bits of paper into a dust pan. His arms reached beyond the too short sleeves of his shirt.

"What is it?" the Father asked.

"Why is that guy working in the rain?"

The Father looked through the window, too. "Francis? Well, I expect he needed to get some fresh air. He's not overly fond of being indoors."

Angie watched the man some more and wondered what it was like not to mind getting wet. When she turned away, she found the Father leaning on his elbows, watching her.

"You pay cash, I'll drop the price a little," she said.

His smile showed tiny uneven teeth. Above them his eyes were warm. "I'm afraid I can only offer something very nominal."

"Like, how much?"

"Can't really say, until I have a look at it."

"Sure. You come by any evening. First-floor apartment, end of the block going that way," she said, tossing her head over her right shoulder.

Three days later Angie came home to find two bags of groceries by her door with a note: *Sorry to have missed you. I'll come again. Father Mulvaney.* She took the bags inside and went through them. One had milk, eggs, butter, bread, frozen pizza, soup cans, spaghetti, even some coffee. In the other were flour, sugar, salt, a bunch of pretty fresh bananas, three oranges, and a can of peaches in heavy syrup.

"Who the fuck wants that shit?" said Kevin. "Why doesn't he just cough up for the piano?"

"He will."

"He better."

That night Kevin was going to rip off Ramon. He'd say to meet him at the bar where Angie worked, and then she'd keep him there with a free drink or two. Angie's boss didn't let her give away drinks. She'd have to put her own money in the till. Kevin didn't think about that. He only had a twenty on him.

"I can make change," she said.

"Forget it, will you?"

Ramon didn't come into the bar at all. Angie called her apartment once, twice. At two a.m. when her shift ended she went home. Marta hadn't been let out. Angie cleaned the dog shit off the floor, walked her around the block, breathed in icy air.

Angie's stomach was tight with hunger. Marta danced when the bowl of dog food descended from Angie's hand.

The phone rang when she was fast asleep.

"Babe, listen, I messed up." He sounded funny. He was crying, she realized.

"What happened, Kev? Where are you?"

"Ramon was there. He tried to get tough." It would have taken a lot more than a slap in the face to put Ramon down. Kevin would have had to finish it.

"Kev, what—"

"I can't believe it. I don't know what the hell happened."

"Where are you?"

"Never mind." He was quiet for a long time.

"Kevin," she said.

"I have to go. Oh, and look in the piano. It's yours." The line went dead.

She got to her feet and padded along the floor. The living room was given over to moonlight from the curtainless window.

The piano lid took some lifting. The envelope inside contained one thousand dollars and the note, *You don't know anything.*

The night was clear, and the violet sky thrown with stars. *Take one down,* her father used to say. *That's what they're there for. Just reach up and take one.*

The morning light seeped over the window ledge, then flowed like clean water into the room. Marta lay warm beside her. Kevin could be anywhere by then, though if Angie guessed right he was at his father's in Indiana, the place he hated so much he described it with a fist to his head—the blue twinkling pool, the big white barn in the middle of fifteen rolling acres, the yellow forsythia hedge. His father would take him in, because money took care of its own. And he'd never get caught, because Ramon was just some drug dealer from Tijuana who'd had nightmares about the truck he crossed the border in, the sealed-up heat of it, the days without water.

Angie opened the kitchen door and let Marta into the little yard to pee. Marta squatted, then ran her nose through the dead winter yard until Angie called her back inside.

After she had dressed and sipped a reheated cup of yesterday's coffee, Angie took Kevin's expensive wool sweaters, heavy flannel shirts, and three pairs of good leather boots and put them in a green garbage bag. She put his books on the sidewalk in front of the house with a note, written on an old grocery sack, *Free.* His toothbrush she threw away. The toothpaste he'd used was hers. She wasn't surprised by the wetness of her eyes, or the tightness in her throat. Ramon had made her feel more at home than Kevin ever had.

Her neighbor, Joey, was sound asleep on a thrown-out sofa two doors down. He wasn't homeless, but seemed to have trouble staying in his apartment at night. Angie nudged him with her foot and he opened his gummy red eyes.

"You want to make twenty bucks?" she asked.

He sat up, spat on the sidewalk, and scratched his head. His fingernails were filthy. "For what?"

"Helping me roll a piano down the block."

"You nuts?"

"You want the money, or not?"

Joey was several inches shorter than Angie, but strong. He had no trouble keeping the piano under control as it rolled back down the ramp. She took the other end and kept it from veering off.

The day was overcast, the air calm. They pushed past parked cars, one with someone asleep in the back seat, another with a broken out windshield, and another up on blocks.

Every few minutes Joey stopped to clear his throat. When they reached the church Angie gave him his twenty.

"How come we brought it here?" he asked.

"That's my business. Now go on."

The front door of the church was locked, and a side door, which gave on the alley between the church and the grocery store next to it, was locked, too. There was a light on the second floor, and Angie threw a pebble at the window there, then another. The window lifted, and Father Mulvaney's head appeared in the open space.

"Who's making that racket?" he called down.

"It's here."

"What is?"

Angie pointed to the piano, which was being closely examined by an old man pushing an empty shopping cart.

"So it is," said the Father.

"It's yours. Free."

"That's most generous of you." The Father's face took on a look of worry as he watched her from above.

"Better get it inside before the weather changes," she said.

"Miss—" But Angie had gone around the corner by then,

back to her apartment. She needed to give Marta another walk after breakfast, get the bag of Kevin's stuff to the thrift shop and take whatever they'd give her in return, then gather up her own things.

Then she'd find a pay phone. The call she gave the police would bring him in. He'd know it was her and one day, if he stopped hating her guts, he might realize that being taken wasn't the same as being bought.

PINNY AND THE FAT GIRL

She was a sullen child, a little slow to catch on, and thus easy to make fun of—*Pinny said two and two is five! And that Miami's the capital of Maine*—the nickname a clever blend of "pinhead" and her real name, Penny. She was tall for her age with light hair some called ash or "dirty" blonde, gray eyes that were green in brighter light, and a clumsy gait because her feet turned in, giving her at times another name—"Pinny pigeon-toes."

She was also an only child. Her mother stayed home and her father sold cars with a flair that should have put him on the stage. Loud suits, loud voice, dropping down to a whisper carefully breathed in the neat pink ear of a lovely young woman needing a car for her new job, or for her life as a new mother, or because she'd finally escaped her wretched marriage and was all on her own.

The flirtation took its toll. Pinny's mother—a snob who always said she'd married down—accused and swore, and then one day announced that she'd had enough, she was not put on this earth to tolerate the disgusting appetites of a fat, balding husband or the glum stupidity of her only child, and off she went, suitcase in hand, leaving Pinny and her father still at the dinner table, their meatloaf greasy and cold.

61

After that, meals were from a can, or Chinese food containers, or pizza boxes, or when necessary, the drugstore where Pinny bought candy with the change her father left on his dresser after having made his own dinner out on pretzels and beer.

Some talked of calling Child Protective Services. One teacher did, and a sallow woman with dark circles below her eyes came to the house unannounced to find Pinny doing laundry and sweeping floors, the father paying bills at the kitchen table, and determined that the pair had formed a good, viable team in the mother's absence.

Pinny didn't mind housework. She didn't mind cooking a fried egg sandwich now and then. She didn't mind her mother being gone, because her mother was often harsh and critical—*No, no, stupid, a minotaur and a centaur are two different things!*—and could really sink a cold finger into Pinny's heart. She didn't mind the way her father's breath smelled when he'd been at the bar, or the jagged sobs he let out some evenings when the twilight was particularly tender and soft.

In fact, just about the only thing she minded was how people treated the fat girl.

The fat girl had transferred from another high school in the middle of the year and often arrived after the last bell. Some said it was because she stayed too long at the breakfast table, and the bus was long gone by the time she waddled out to find it. The truth was that she had a little brother to dress and feed, and a barn to muck out, with her big rubber boots still on to prove it. She smelled funny, like earth and sweat and something sweet—like hand soap she would later say, a cheap scent of honey and lemon.

One thing was sure—the fat girl knew how to make an entrance. She took her time crossing the classroom to her seat by the window, looking at the faces turned her way as if they were all her loving fans.

The fat girl's name was Eunice, and hearing it called out by the homeroom teacher made the other students roar. A person couldn't help the name she was given—like Penny, for Penelope and her mother's passion for all things ancient Greek—any more than she could help smelling weird or being fat. Pinny was soon a quick defender of the fat girl— *Oh, yeah? Well, you're ugly, how about that?*—sometimes with a raised fist though she had never actually hit anyone.

"You don't need to stick up for me," the fat girl told Pinny one day. "Not that I don't appreciate it, but I got some ideas of my own on how to fix these losers."

Not long after that a boy opening his locker was met with a rotten egg smeared on photographs of racing cars taped lovingly to the inside of the door. This boy had been a principal teaser of the fat girl only days before, taunting her in the lunchroom as she ate her two bologna sandwiches, one cheese sandwich, and several cookies, calling her *Blimpo* and *Miss Piggy*. A pretty girl who'd told the fat girl she smelled like a used Kotex found exactly that in her locker the following morning.

After school, the fat girl took a bus that drove sixteen winding miles through the farmland of upstate New York to deposit her at an intersection of two country roads. She walked along the one that bore east until its cracked pavement turned to gravel and then to dirt, to arrive at her house, a two-story wooden structure that must have been very beautiful about seventy-five years ago. The porch wrapped around three sides, the peak had a lightning rod with a ball of purple glass on top, and the windows were framed with shutters. The paint had long since worn away, and the bare wood stood against the revolving seasons like a tired, old face. She lived there with both of her parents and the baby brother, just a year and a half old. The father had a herd of dairy cows whose milk brought in some income, otherwise he worked for Tompkins County repairing roads. The mother sometimes waited tables at a bar six miles away and was rumored to have a boyfriend over in Slaterville Springs, an ex-con named Lyal who sometimes sold a hot stereo or a shotgun from the back of his mobile home.

One Friday afternoon, Pinny rode the bus home with the fat girl. Their walk to the house was colored with the green light of newly leafing trees.

"It's nice out here," Pinny told the fat girl.

"It bites. I'd rather live where you do."

Pinny lived in "the flats," or downtown Dunston, near a creek that ran noisily in summer and froze over in the winter.

"No, you wouldn't. The college kids hit the bars, then wander around singing and shouting like a bunch of retards. It's a pain," said Pinny.

The fat girl breathed loudly as she walked, her thick arms swung wide with the effort of moving her forward, and her backpack thumped and rustled with the rhythm of her stride.

The fat girl's mother was sitting on the porch with a pan and a plastic bag of green beans. With a small knife she removed the end of each bean, threw it into the yard, snapped the bean in two, and dropped the pieces in the pan at her feet. She had the same yellow hair the fat girl had, but not as bright and shiny.

She looked at Pinny.

"Who's this?" she asked.

"A friend from school," said the fat girl.

"Hello, friend from school."

Pinny watched the fat girl's mother work her beans.

"Go on in and get something to eat if you want. There's lemonade and Ding Dongs," the fat girl's mother said.

The house smelled of fried fish and sour milk. A television set was on in another room playing what sounded like a game show. The fat girl dropped her backpack on the kitchen floor, helped herself to the contents of the white cardboard box on the counter, then went to the refrigerator and drank lemonade right from the pitcher. Pinny put her backpack in the corner by the door they'd come in through. In another corner was a playpen, and in the playpen the fat girl's little brother was moving a red plastic train back and forth on bright green wheels. His yellow hair was cut so short it was a light fuzz on his head. There was a pink Band-Aid stuck to his scalp that was black and sticky-looking along its edge.

He looked up and wailed.

"Stick it, Zach," the fat girl said. Zach kept up his wail. The mother called, "See to him, Eunice, will you?"

The fat girl lifted Zach from the pen. He turned to Pinny and watched her with huge blue eyes.

"He's pretty," said Pinny.

"Handsome, you mean."

Pinny shrugged. Boys could be pretty just the way girls could. There was a boy in her English class who was very pretty, small-boned and delicate. He was from India. His parents taught at the university. His skin was coffee-colored, and his hair was black. Kids called him "faggot" and "homo," which made no sense, because he didn't seem to like boys more than he liked girls. He didn't seem to like anyone.

The fat girl returned Zach to the pen, and then showed Pinny her room. It was bigger than Pinny's with three tall windows so dirty the sunlight was dim. On a shelf over the bed was a row of glass dolphins. The fat girl said she loved dolphins because they were smart and helped people. Pinny's mother liked dolphins, too, and had had a small golden one on a bracelet that Pinny said she'd be wearing herself right now if her mother hadn't taken it with her.

"Where did she go?" asked the fat girl.

"A friend's."

"Why?"

"My dad sort of has a thing for other women."

"You hear from her?"

"Sometimes."

Pinny's mother called home once a week to update Pinny's father on the progress she was making with the injustice she'd suffered. Sometimes she wanted to talk to Pinny and Pinny managed to listen and say little. *Fine* was her answer to every question which made her mother say, *Well, I see you haven't broadened your horizons much in my absence.* Pinny's mother was living in Connecticut with her college roommate, also separated from her husband. She said they had great times, ladies out on the town, but Pinny could tell her mother found it boring and probably wanted to come home. Pinny's father wasn't asking her to anymore, not the way he had the winter before, around the holidays, and Pinny's mother hinted that she might return before the end of the summer, if *things improved.* Pinny didn't know what things she referred to, and knew better than to ask.

The days got long and warm and school was as dull as toast. There was nothing to pay attention to and nothing to get upset about.

Then the fat girl fell in love. The boy was Carl Pratt, and Pinny saw nothing remarkable about him, except that he was skinny and tall and threw a good softball in gym class.

"You're nuts," the fat girl said. "He's totally hot. And I think he likes me." Carl Pratt looked at Pinny, not at the fat girl when they were together. Pinny had gotten very curvy in the last year, and when Carl Pratt smiled, he was smiling at Pinny and Pinny knew it, so she tried to discourage the fat girl's passion for Carl Pratt, saying he was a geek, he had greasy hair, he didn't know how to tie his own shoes. The proof of that were the gray laces that flopped by his huge feet as he took himself at full tilt down the hall, his notebook pressed flat against his hard thigh, and his pen balanced with the grace of a feather behind his ear.

After making eyes at Pinny for two whole weeks, Carl Pratt appeared at her locker, put his hand firmly on her back and said, "You're awfully sweet, you know that?" Her response was a solid blow to his upper arm, which made him gaze down at her with pure adoration before wandering away.

When the fat girl realized that Carl Pratt actually liked Pinny, she was driven to bitter weeping, and flung herself down on Pinny's bed so hard the springs creaked and the headboard slapped the wall. Her milk white arms raised above her head in a gesture of defeat and she said, "I'm going to take a header off the bridge."

There were several bridges in Dunston to choose from, all built across a deep section of gorge. People committed suicide by jumping from them every year, usually students from the Ivy League university when semester grades were posted. Locals didn't jump. They shot themselves, or were found hanging from a barn beam, or on the floor with an empty bottle of sleeping pills.

"Bull," said Pinny. The fat girl looked at her with wet eyes and howled with misery. By the time she stopped crying, the light had died in the spring sky and Pinny's father called up the stairs to ask what was for dinner.

Pinny fried some hot dogs in a pan and heated a can of yellow corn. She put slices of bread in the toaster and spread peanut butter on them. Her father and the fat girl ate their food without a word. Then her father looked at the fat girl and asked, "Who's the fella?"

"What fella?" asked Pinny.

"The one who's got her down in the dumps, of course."

Pinny said Carl Pratt's name.

"Pratt. Father's Don Pratt? Sold him a Buick last year. Good car. Wouldn't go for the extended warranty. Only a couple hundred bucks more. Just couldn't talk him into it."

The fat girl wiped her nose on a paper napkin.

"Well, it's his loss," she said. Pinny wasn't sure if the fat girl meant Carl Pratt or his father, but the statement worked, either way.

Pinny asked Carl Pratt to be nice to the fat girl as a favor to her.

"What, are you kidding?" he asked. They were in the gym where basketball practice had just ended and Carl Pratt was gathering up basketballs.

"She really likes you."

"Gross."

"You're mean."

"Not to you, I'm not." And then he kissed Pinny right on the lips. She thought it was the most disgusting thing she'd ever done and that she'd probably never kiss anyone again as long as she lived. But, since Carl Pratt seemed to like it so much, Pinny soon learned she could get what she wanted letting him have his way. The next day Carl Pratt said "Hi" to the fat girl, and even managed a weak smile in her direction. For that Pinny paid him with two kisses.

Day by day Carl Pratt paid attention to the fat girl, causing a huge stir. Though he had a reputation as a ladies' man, his interest in the fat girl still couldn't be fathomed. Someone said Josh Silverman, one of the wealthier students who'd spent money on gags before, was up to his old tricks. What a good joke it would be to build up the fat girl, only to let her down, everyone said.

Pinny kept the truth quiet by letting Carl Pratt kiss her for up to an hour, often with his hands inside her shirt. She liked it a little better than she used to, but still not too much.

"Do you kiss her, too?" Pinny asked. The fat girl didn't say what she did with Carl Pratt after school at his house while his father sold insurance and his mother slept off her night shift at the hospital. She just drifted around with a quiet light in her eyes, and a rosy glow on her round, smooth cheeks.

"Not like this," said Carl Pratt.

Pinny hadn't really thought that Carl Pratt kissed the fat girl. She had expected him to say no, she realized. She had gotten the idea that all they did was talk, because Carl Pratt had once said, "Man, she talks a lot."

Pinny was deeply jealous of the fat girl, because all of a sudden she, too, had fallen for Carl Pratt.

She refused to let either the fat girl or Carl Pratt know. When the fat girl talked about him, her voice all soft and dewy, Pinny listened with a blank face and an occasional nod. After school, on the days when the fat girl had to go straight home and had waved goodbye to him from the pushed down window of the school bus, he'd find Pinny, take her behind the building and she wouldn't lean into his kisses no matter how much she wanted to. When he finally pulled away, she made her hands let go and not clutch his hard shoulders.

One afternoon, with the end of the year only eight days away, Carl Pratt wanted to go home with Pinny after school. The fat girl had left early for a dental appointment, but Pinny still didn't think it was a good idea. The fat girl might call and she'd feel weird about answering the phone. If she didn't answer, the fat girl's voice on the machine would be hard to hear. But since there was no good way to explain this to Carl Pratt, she agreed.

A little while later, as Pinny led Carl up her back stairs, she suddenly stopped. "What?" he said.

She turned around and looked down at him from two steps above.

"You said you dad's at work, right?" he said.

She nodded.

"So don't worry, okay?" He stroked her arm and she shivered. She was afraid he wouldn't like her room, that he would think it too girly. The princess costume her mother had bought her for Halloween when she was four years old was tacked to the wall above her bed. The thought of her mother seeing her that way—as a princess—if only that once sometimes made her sad. Pinny had gone from not caring that her mother was gone to caring more than made sense, and somehow that sadness she felt—that deep longing—was all to do with Carl Pratt.

Carl Pratt didn't say anything about the costume, or the flowery scarf she had across her lamp, or the rocking chair, or the stuffed yellow mouse in the corner. He put down his backpack and took her in his arms.

A few moments later they were lying on her bed and he was wrestling with her shirt.

"Stop it."

"Come on." He stopped. Then he said, "Let's screw."

"It's dangerous."

"No, it's not."

Pinny lay in a state that swung between fear and joy like the heavy brass pendulum of the clock downstairs. To stop that swing she held Carl Pratt's hand and squeezed hard.

"I don't want to get pregnant," she said

He let go of her hand. "You won't."

"Why not?"

"Well, because thin girls like you don't get pregnant very fast. It takes a long time."

The sound of Pinny's father's car in the driveway ended the conversation. They were sitting side by side with a science book between them when her father came into her room to say hello.

Pinny introduced Carl Pratt to her father, and upon

hearing the name he gave Pinny a good hard look, and went downstairs to watch television.

"You better go," Pinny told Carl Pratt.

Over dinner Pinny's father sipped his beer and watched Pinny eat the fried chicken he'd bought. His bright blue tie had a grease stain Pinny couldn't help staring at.

"Honey, about this boy. I'm not the best one to give advice in matters of the heart, obviously, but you should be careful about who you spend time with. No good making people jealous," he said.

Pinny saw her father thinking about her mother, who had sent him a letter saying she might have been wrong, too harsh, too quick to judge, but that she still doubted his strength to resist the siren call of the young and restless, mixing mythology with a stupid soap opera in a way that made Pinny wonder who was dumber than whom.

"We're just friends. He helps me with my homework," Pinny said.

"Good."

That weekend the fat girl called and said she knew damn well Carl Pratt didn't really like her and only invited her over when he wanted to cop a feel.

"But that's OK, it's payback time," she said, with a sniff.

"What do you mean?"

"You'll see." The fat girl hung up.

Monday and Tuesday dragged by. Carl Pratt was busy with basketball, and the fat girl was sullen.

On Wednesday, the last day of school, the fat girl appeared with her hair short and spiky. The nine inches she'd cut off herself were stuffed in a plastic bag, which she handed to Carl Pratt in front of a crowd of people and said, "This is the only thing you ever liked about me, so here, keep it."

Someone grabbed the bag, and when the fat girl reached for it, the bag was thrown from hand to hand, always above her head. "Here, Fat Girl," and "Hey, Fat Girl, over here," people called.

The fat girl brought her fists to her face and screamed. A teacher emerged from an open door, everyone scattered, and Pinny didn't see the fat girl again all day.

After the last bell rang Carl Pratt found Pinny waiting by the fat girl's locker. "She's not here," he said. "I think she skipped out."

"Because those kids were so mean to her."

Carl shrugged.

"I should have stopped them," said Pinny.

"You? How?"

"I don't know."

Pinny stared down at Carl Pratt's sockless feet, stuck inside his big, torn sneakers. She was to blame, for wanting Carl Pratt to be nice to the fat girl in the first place. She hadn't seen how stupid it was to ask someone to fake what he didn't feel. But even if he'd felt nothing, and hadn't liked her at all, not one bit, he should have felt bad for the way she'd been teased. Pinny wanted him to, if only a little.

"Carl—"

"Look. I have something fucked up to tell you. I'm going to California for the summer," he said.

Pinny lifted her eyes and stared firmly into his.

"I got a cousin there, a park ranger. My folks think he'll make me straighten up and get all serious about school," he said.

Carl's grades sucked, everyone knew that. He was in Pinny's math class, and she couldn't believe some of the things he didn't get. Carl Pratt looked at his watch.

"Crap. My mother wants to take me to get a haircut. I have to go," he said.

He pressed a small gold chain into her hand and said to wear it around her neck every day until he returned. There was a metal heart hanging on the chain with his name engraved. Pinny looked at the chain, her throat heavy and tight. Then Carl Pratt trotted off, his back pack bouncing on his bony shoulder.

Pinny left the building and walked slowly home. The air smelled of the season to come. Hollyhocks would climb below her dining room window, flies would buzz against the screens, the air would be as still as glass. Her mother would be in Connecticut, drinking her iced tea in a different back yard, Carl would be climbing mountains out west, and Pinny would be there, in boring old Dunston, thinking about both of them.

The fat girl was sitting on the front porch of Pinny's house eating a candy bar and sipping soda pop through a bright pink straw. Pinny slipped the chain that was still in her hand into her pocket.

"Where have you been?" the fat girl asked, chewing.

"Nowhere."

"I skipped the rest of the day."

"I know. It won't matter now. The year's over."

The fat girl ran her fingers through her hair. "It feels weird," she said. "Like my head's too light."

"Was it hard to cut it by yourself?"

"Yeah."

"I'd have helped you."

"You'd have told me not to."

Pinny pushed a candy wrapper off the step and sat next to the fat girl.

"Carl Pratt's going to California for the summer," said Pinny.

"Really? How do you know?"

"Someone at school said so."

"Well, I say good riddance, Fuck Face."

Pinny wanted to explain about her and Carl Pratt, to clear the air and let her know what to expect when he came back and school started again in the fall, but didn't see how. The truth was that she'd gone behind the fat girl's back.

"Let's take a walk," said Pinny.

"Okay."

They watched their shadows move along the slate sidewalk, Pinny's so long and thin and the fat girl's a bobbing circle. Where the road began its steep climb to campus, a waterfall spilled over thin shelves of rock. A footpath ran along one side of the falls, and Pinny led them up slowly to give the fat girl time to catch her breath.

They reached a level spot on the path and stopped to watch the water rush and spray. They leaned against the metal rail in silence. The fat girl's face was in shadow.

"He wanted me to go all the way, you know, and I wouldn't. He said, 'What do you have to lose, you're just a fat girl.'"

Pinny's cheeks got hot, a lot hotter than the afternoon's eighty-five degrees would cause.

"He's a jerk," said Pinny.

The fat girl took a candy bar out of her backpack, unwrapped it, and bit off the end.

"I mean, it's not like I love being like this. I've tried to lose weight about a million times," she said.

"What about those programs where you drop twenty pounds in two months?" asked Pinny.

"They cost money. And then you have to pay for food."

"My mother once lost thirty pounds all on her own. Try eating a lot of protein, or slashing your carbohydrates for a while."

The fat girl stopped eating and stared at the water. Then she turned to Pinny with an eager gleam in her eye.

"Tell me something," she said.

"What?"

"Why do you act dumb, when you're not?"

"I don't."

"Come on. Remember that one day at lunch, when someone said, 'Irregardless of that,' you said to me, 'It's *regardless!'* And in History that time, when Mr. Cain called on you and asked who the fifth president of the United States was, you said you didn't know but I saw you had James Monroe in your notebook with a big circle around his name."

Pinny watched the water run. She didn't know what to say. Playing dumb was something she'd learned to do long ago, maybe as a defense against her mother's constant disappointment in her.

"I don't like people bugging me. If they think I'm dumb, they leave me alone," Pinny said.

"Don't you hate getting bad grades when you can get good ones?"

"I don't care about grades."

"How about being treated like an idiot?"

Pinny shrugged.

"Melissa Franks called you a moron when you answered wrong in Spanish, and you got all red in the face. You dug your nails in your palm. I saw the marks," the fat girl said.

She had a point, Pinny thought. A good one, too. She did hate being treated like an idiot, especially by Carl Pratt. *You won't get pregnant. It takes longer with thin girls.* After sitting in the same health class with her, hearing the same words from their teacher, he still thought she didn't get it. In a way it was her fault for playing the part so well, but if he'd cared—really cared—he'd have raised the issue first.

"What are you doing?" the fat girl asked. Pinny had just taken Carl Pratt's chain out of her pocket and thrown it into the falls.

"Making a wish. A reverse wish. To fix something I shouldn't have done."

"What?"

"Well, if I tell you, it'll hang on me forever."

They started back down. Pinny remembered a little blue stone bracelet she'd once found in a store. It was the prettiest thing she'd ever seen. She'd begged and begged for it, and her mother said it would get lost, or broken, and wasn't the kind of thing a child should wear. She'd cried for weeks and then one day she just didn't care about it anymore. Maybe that would happen with Carl Pratt. Maybe all of a sudden the ache for him would just go away.

The fat girl looked miserable. She had a film of sweat on her face that she wiped away with the back of one hand. Then she stopped walking and pinched her stomach.

"Know what?" she said.

"What?"

"I'm really sick of candy." She removed the last bar she had in her backpack and threw it into the street where it got flattened by a car few minutes later. That made them laugh so hard their eyes got wet.

They laughed a lot that summer; at the way the stylist looked at the fat girl's hair when she went to get it done; at the fat girl's little brother who learned to talk in complete, bossy sentences; about the tie Pinny's father bought with pink and yellow dots. In quieter moments, as they reviewed the year behind and looked to the year ahead, they promised never to be Pinny and the fat girl again but only Penny and Eunice, and the whole time, as the heat rose and then fell, they didn't mention Carl Pratt once.

ALL THE ROADS
THAT LEAD FROM HOME

A silent winter gave way to a violent spring. Shouts, slammed doors, then tears and bitter questions. *Are you saying she's better than I am? Are you?*

Finally my father left with his suitcase, and my mother went to lie down. Like she did all those times we were supposed to go to the lake for a picnic, right at the last minute, after I'd changed into my suit and he was already in the car, waiting. I'd go out and say it was off, and he'd put the sandwiches he'd made back in the refrigerator and go grade some more papers.

Such was our life in Dunston—that town on a Finger Lake. With an Ivy League school. High above blah blah blah's waters.

They both taught there. So did all the nerds they tried to impress with their dumb cocktail parties, where my mother never sulked, but chatted and flitted about like a nervous squirrel.

And for what? Guys with chalky hands, wild hair, and crooked glasses sitting on the couch, glad for the drink and bowl of nuts, talking their crap. *Dartmouth made him an offer, don't you know?*

Good for Dartmouth. No one ever made me an offer,

only a demand—*Amelia, go look for my slip in the dryer*, and *Call my secretary and tell her to cancel my lecture. I can't teach those morons anything, anyway.*

With my father gone, and money a problem, the idea of getting canned was usually enough to get her on her feet. Then she stared a long time in the bathroom mirror, and moaned about how awful she looked. She started wearing mascara and eye shadow that made her look like a beat-up freak; floppy skirts, bright beads, long sweaters that hung down to mid-thigh.

When I described all this to my friend, Giselle, she said, "She's just trying to escape."

"From what?"

"How lame she really is."

That same day a guy showed up to take my mother riding on the back of his motorcycle.

"It's absolutely amazing, darling! Really! All that guff about the wind in your hair, well, it's all true," she said, after he'd roared away again. She smelled like aftershave and gasoline. "Oh, by the way, he runs that shoe store downtown, you know the one, Cosantinis?"

Motorcycle Man improved her attitude so much she burbled through her lectures on the bloody battles of the American Civil War, and even did a little soft shoe now and then to amuse her students. The ones who weren't amused complained to the department chairman, and my mother was asked to consider all the eager young beavers ready to take her place. "So, you know what I did?" she asked me. "This." She shoved out her top teeth and gnawed the air. The chairman told this to another professor, who told his secretary, who told my father's secretary, who told my father that same afternoon, because even though everyone knew he'd moved out, it was still sort of assumed he'd want to keep an eye on her. That Sunday he took me out for ice cream, bought me vanilla although my favorite was chocolate, and asked, "So, kiddo, how are things at home? Everything okay with You Know Who?"

I stared out the tall, dusty window at Route 13. A truck with the name *Bradford*, a department store in Syracuse where my mother once took me to shop, rolled through the green light and picked up speed as it gained the hill. I pushed back my plastic cup of sloshy ice cream which said *Betty Lou's Sweets and Treats* in thick blue script.

"I think she's having a mid-life crisis," I said.

He pulled thoughtfully on the beard he'd grown to impress his girlfriend. "That's what she always accused me of having."

School ended for the year. My report card saying I was in the ninety-sixth percentile of my tenth-grade class got me a card from my father with a five-dollar bill inside. Then he took the girlfriend camping in Minnesota.

"Minnesota? Who the hell goes to Minnesota, for Christ's sake?" my mother said.

"That's where he's from."

"The man's insane."

I poured her another glass of iced tea. She stared at it, drank some, then gave me a hard, probing look. "Are you all right, Amelia?" she asked.

"Why?"

"I don't know. You've been acting strange lately."

"No, I haven't."

"Well, there's definitely something different about you."

No shit, Sherlock! My whole life was different. One day everything's fine, the next my father leaves, and my mother gets even weirder.

"What about that little friend of yours, Genevieve?" my mother said.

"Giselle. What about her?"

"Why don't you call her up, get together. It's nice to be with someone your own age."

"She went to France for the summer with her family."

"Isn't *she* a lucky girl." In another minute my mother would say how much she wished she could go somewhere fun, too, and probably never would, now that she was on her own and struggling to make ends meet, so I went back to the safety of my room and *Anna Karenina*. Now, *there* was someone who had it tough.

My mother saw a lot of Motorcycle Man when she wasn't teaching summer school. His name was Harv, short for Harvey. He took her dancing at a bar that played country music. When they got bored with dancing they went bowling. When Harv slipped a disk, my mother went to his house every day and made him dinner.

Then, during the weeks on his back, with nothing to do but think, he decided he'd wasted his life. He'd always wanted to paint, and when he got on his feet he sold his motorcycle, bought a van and drove to California with a bunch of blank canvases. It all took him less than a week.

"First your father, and now Harv. Just like that." My mother snapped her fingers. "I'm just not *interesting* enough. I'm not enough *fun*." She rattled the ice in her glass of tea and examined the fingernails of her left hand. "I've got a lot more to offer than they think, and I can prove it, too."

Later that week I found her in the guest room, hanging a new pair of curtains. The shorts she wore revealed a network of red blue veins on the backs of her thighs, like a road map.

"Here, hold that hem up for me," she said.

"What's wrong with the old curtains?"

"These are brighter and much more cheerful." They were ugly was what they were, decorated with daisies and some orange flower I didn't recognize. My mother got off the stepladder, stood back, and admired them.

"I'm sure she'll like them," she said.

"Who?"

"The girl who'll be staying with us for a while."

"What girl? What are you talking about?"

"A nice sixteen-year-old. She's been having a little trouble at home, and we're going to try to help her."

"But—"

"Her mother remarried and she's had some difficulty adjusting to a new person in her life, I guess. She goes to Martha's church, the mother, I mean, and they got to talking. Martha said we had some extra room, and suggested the daughter stay here for a little while, to give everyone a break, as it were."

Martha was my mother's oldest friend, and one of the few people who called regularly after my father left. She was one of the do-gooder types, always meddling in other people's problems. She'd come by our house more than once to look at me like something under a microscope and ask how I was bearing up, if I was spending enough time with friends.

"And you just said 'yes?'" I asked.

"Of course. Why not?"

"Because I don't want anyone moving in!"

"Oh, honestly, Amelia! You need to be more flexible, and accept new situations with a positive attitude."

Uh, huh. Just yesterday we saw my father's girlfriend in the grocery store buying a frozen leg of lamb. My mother said she'd like to give her a good beating with it, and wasn't exactly quiet about it, either.

"It'll be good for you, having someone to talk to. And even if you don't like her, I expect you to be pleasant," she said.

Suddenly I felt tired, so tired I could lie down on the newly made bed and sleep for about a year.

"Does this someone have a name?"

"Mary."

She got out of the car, a beat-up station wagon with twine around the front bumper, wearing a sleeveless blouse and a skirt, as if she were going to a job interview. Her suitcase had brown tape along the sides. The driver of the car was a big man in a jean jacket. His hair looked wet and shiny in the sun. When he tried to hug her goodbye she pulled away. He seemed angry until he saw my mother coming down the walk. He stepped back, grinned, and offered his hand. Mary saw me standing on the porch, in front of the open door. She approached carrying her suitcase, looking at the ground.

I thought of the things I didn't want her touching, like my silver dollar from 1922, or the turquoise watch fob that had belonged to my great-grandfather, and of course all my books, though she didn't look like the kind of person who'd care much for books. Her makeup had a distinctly orange tint, and her hair had tiny flakes of dandruff scattered along her crown.

She followed me across the screened-in porch, through the French doors into the living room, and stopped in front of my father's grand piano.

"Who plays?" she asked.

"No one."

"Maybe I'll learn." No fucking way! I didn't want to listen to her mindless plunking. It was bad enough having her here. I stared at her feet. Her running shoes were filthy and she didn't have socks on.

She said, "Look, I know my being here wasn't your idea and—"

"It's fine."

I brought her down the hall, and opened the door to her room. It stank of the air freshener my mother had sprayed earlier. Mary put her suitcase down, went to the window, and looked out to where the man was still talking to my mother. She kept watch until the car drove away. A few seconds later my mother opened the door.

"Fabulous! You're all settled in!"

"Yes, ma'am. Thank you," said Mary.

"Oh, for Heaven's sake! No one ever calls me 'Ma'am.' Joan will do fine." My mother stood there, smiling like a feeb. "Your stepfather seems awfully nice. He hopes you'll be comfortable here with us, but that you won't stay away too long. I think he misses you already." When she got no answer, she said, "Well, I'll just leave you two alone to get acquainted," and flounced out.

Mary flopped down on the bed, threw her arms above her head, and stared at the ceiling. The stubble in her armpits was like tiny black seeds.

"Dinner's at six," I said, and closed the door as quietly as I could.

We established a routine. Mary made breakfast, I got my mother up and off to campus. After breakfast I did the dishes and went into my room to read. Mary rode my old bicycle to the store with money my mother left taped on the TV. I did laundry in the afternoon, and Mary cleaned house. When my mother came home Mary made dinner. At first I didn't help her, then my mother made me. "Can't you see how lonely she is?" she hissed. "Go on, now, and try to *make friends*." The kitchen was small, and Mary's thick, sad body made it smaller. By then I'd come to wonder about the scar on her left hand, a small, white crescent, like a moon in the morning sky. I watched it rise and fall along the counter top, in and out of the dishwasher, on the handle of the refrigerator, up to a stray hair she pushed behind her ear.

All we said to each other were things like, "Here's the frying pan," and, "Where do you guys keep the paper towels?" At table my mother tried to draw her out. "You're a good cook, Mary. Did you learn that at home?" and, "My, the way you ride that bike all over tells me you're used to hard exercise. Isn't that so?"

Mary just shrugged, which I could tell pissed my mother off. She wanted gushing thanks for being allowed to stay in such a nice house, in such a nice neighborhood, with such nice, nice people. When Martha called to see how things were going, my mother said, "Oh, fine, I suppose. Certainly hasn't learned the art of conversation, though, has she?"

When the novelty of Mary wore off and life got back to normal—a new normal, I mean—my mother went back to moping, usually in the late afternoons.

"Thing is, guy dumps you, all you can do is say, 'Later, Slick,'" said Mary one afternoon, peering at the pimply chicken she'd put in the oven.

"Two guys. The second one moved to California."

"Yeah, why?"

"To be an artist or something."

"The creep who hooked my mom thought he can write poems. As if."

Her face was hard. She peeled potatoes slowly, lifting the skin from each as if she wanted it to bleed. She'd been here for three whole weeks, I realized. When she wasn't doing chores, she stayed in her room and played solitaire with a grubby deck of cards she'd brought with her.

"Better spill it," she said.

"What?"

"Whatever's on your mind." She pulled a piece of potato skin from the blades of the peeler and dropped it in the trash can below the sink. I waited for her to look at me. She didn't.

"Okay. What was so bad about living at home?" I asked.

Mary put the peeler on the counter and faced me, hands on hips. One of her blue eyes had a splash of yellow I hadn't noticed before, like a single flame. She stepped toward me and pinched my right boob, hard.

"Ouch!"

"That. He done it to me over and over, then he done a few other things I don't need to show you."

My boob throbbed. "Didn't you tell someone?"

"Like who? My mom's so in love with the jerk, she'd never believe me."

"What about the police?"

"Sure. I can't prove shit."

"Didn't you at least try?" The flame in her eye didn't seem quite as fierce.

"No."

"You should. He'd get in a lot of trouble. He could even go to jail."

"He could. Only what would my mom do then? She can't go one day without a man to hang her arms around."

My mother stood in the doorway to the kitchen in a tight pair of jeans and a lace underwire bra. In her hand she had a sweater I'd put in the wash. "This goes to the dry cleaner! How many times must I say the same thing?"

"I'm sorry," I said.

"It's all well and good to be sorry, but here's my sweater, all shrunken down like an African head."

She held it out to me, a pink fuzzball that was always too tight, even when it was new.

"Maybe the dry cleaner can do something with it," I said.

"Not unless he's a bloody magician."

"Maybe you can buy another one."

"As if money just grows on trees." She sighed and went upstairs to her bedroom. Mary looked at me and shook her head.

"No wonder your old man split. No offense," she said.

"He left because he found someone else."

"Yeah, but why was he even looking?"

For all the reasons I'd never told anyone and suddenly wanted to tell her, like how my mother rode my toy rocking horse in front of company once, and hosted an elegant party in bare feet, and answered the door wearing a shower cap she'd forgotten to take off. Mary laughed, the first time she had since coming here, and went on laughing, even after my mother slammed her door against the noise.

August came, and with it my mother's birthday. Mary baked a cake and decorated it with sloppy pink hearts. My mother stared at it a while before saying, "Thank you," and then asked me to give her just a tiny slice. Mary and I were both on our second piece when the phone rang.

"Hey, kiddo," he said, when I picked up. "Thought I oughtta call and wish You Know Who a happy birthday. She there?"

"It's Dad," I said, my hand over the receiver.

I could see her thinking she might just refuse to speak to him, then she took the phone into her room. They didn't talk long. I was sure she told him it was time to come to his senses and to stop all this nonsense, and from how bummed she was afterwards—so much that she lay down on the couch with a cold rag on her head—I knew he wasn't coming to anything, and certainly not home.

I put the dishes away, then found Mary in her room, reading a fashion magazine. She'd rearranged the furniture a few days before. The bed wasn't in front of the window any more, but facing it, so she could see outside the minute she opened her eyes.

"She down again?" she asked.

I nodded and sat in the rocking chair we'd gotten from the attic. I thought about my dad. I'd seen him only twice since school ended. He'd driven by a couple of times with his girlfriend. They'd bought a house a few blocks away, a short walk, if an invitation ever came. As for Mary, she hadn't had a single phone call from her mother in all the weeks she'd been there, which bugged her, I think, but also made her glad, because then they couldn't talk about her going back home.

"That's a nice dress," Mary said, showing me the picture she meant.

"It's OK, I guess."

"You don't like clothes, much, do you?"

I shrugged. I usually wore T-shirts and blue jeans.

"I love 'em," said Mary. "I should learn how to sew, make up some of my own." Her own clothes looked like shit, the kind of stuff you found in thrift stores, lots of polyester and puffed sleeves.

"Be nice to have something new for the first day of school," she said.

"Don't remind me about school."

"Only a couple weeks off, now." She looked at me suddenly.

"What?" I said.

"Bet you she didn't sign me up."

"Who?"

"Your mom. That weird friend of hers said if I was still living here in August, then I'd have to go to your school, on account of the one I went to last year's about twenty miles off, and the bus probably won't come all that way just for me."

"Shit!"

"I got an idea. Call the school, pretend to be her, and say you want me to go there. Say we've become real good friends, and that you don't want to split us up."

"Why can't you?"

"Because I don't talk fancy enough."

I'd have said no except that the flame in her eye had gone all wobbly when she asked me.

The next morning, with Mary beside me, I took a deep breath and picked up the phone.

"Yes, I realize time is running short, but surely you still

have room? She's had the most difficult time, poor thing. I'd hate to do anything that would impede the fine progress she's making," I said. The secretary agreed to mail the required paperwork, and said I'd have to provide a copy of Mary's birth certificate when I sent it back.

"We have a problem," I said, when I got off the phone.

"Yeah, what?"

"They want a copy of your birth certificate."

"I got it."

"You do?"

"Hey, once I learned I was getting sprung outta there, I took everything I might ever need. Even my book of what you call it, from the doctor, vaccinations."

She grinned. Her hair was clean, with no dandruff at all. And she'd stopped wearing that awful makeup. I was glad to see her look more like herself, like a girl who'd do fine at my sort of snotty school. We made a plan to get her some new clothes downtown with a credit card my mother never used. If that worked, maybe we could get her a decent haircut, too.

Four days later Harv appeared at the front door in a T-shirt, Bermuda shorts, and sandals. His toenails were thick and yellow. Mary saw them, too. She caught my eye as he made his way across the living room to my mother's shriek and outstretched arms.

"What in the world are *you* doing here?" she asked.

"Seeing you."

"But—"

"Can't paint worth a damn, babe. And that's the truth."

They set up in the back yard with a pitcher of martinis my mother made and spent the rest of the afternoon getting smashed. Mary and I ordered a pizza and ate it her room with a dusty fan I'd found in the basement. Then we watched an old movie on TV about some nutty woman who finds religion and blows off her family so she can do good works for everybody else.

The next day was Sunday. After the martinis my mother and Harv had gone out somewhere and come home late. His van was still in the driveway.

Mary was outside, looking up. The sky was silver and the air still.

"Looks like we had company last night," she said, when I joined her.

"Yeah."

"They make noise?"

"Not that I heard."

"Lucky you. Nothing worse than hearing people fuck. You wouldn't believe the racket in my mom's room, once Romeo moved in."

We heard someone slamming the kitchen cabinets, and went in to see. It was Harv, still in his shorts, and an old T-shirt of my father's that had bright blue paint stains on the front.

He looked at us with bloodshot eyes. "Hey, there. Either of you girls know how to make coffee?"

"Just instant," said Mary. That was a lie. She made my mother freshly ground coffee every morning. She put the kettle on to boil without looking at Harv. She brought down an ancient jar of instant coffee, set it on the counter by Harv's car keys and said, "Spoons are in there, sugar's over there, three scoops and you're good to go."

I followed her into her room. She opened the window with a single, sharp push.

"What's wrong with you?" I asked.

"Him. He got no business coming around."

"Maybe not, but he's here."

She sat on her bed, and studied the braided rug. "Nothing pisses you off, does it?" she said.

"What the hell's that supposed to mean?"

"Your folks split up. Your dad hangs out with some young chick, your mom turns into a three-year-old, then this clown shows up and acts like he owns the damn place." Her face was full of color. She went on staring at the rug. Thunder boomed in the distance, and a slow breeze came in through the window screen. In the kitchen Harv banged one drawer, then another, looking for the spoons Mary had already pointed out.

"Christ!" she said, and stood up.

"I'll do it," I said. I went out and found a spoon. I poured him his water, stirred the coffee in, and put it on the kitchen table. He sat down.

"You wouldn't have any cream and sugar around, would you?" he asked. I passed him the sugar bowl, and got the carton of cream from the refrigerator. Mary was wrong. Harv pissed me off plenty, wanting me to wait on him like that.

He sipped his coffee, and stared at it oddly. My mother came down the stairs slowly, holding hard onto the hand rail. She looked sick, as if she had the flu or something.

"What the hell are you drinking?" she asked Harv.

"Coffee."

She took his cup, and examined it. "Oh, darling, you'll have to do better than that if I'm coming on board." She ruffled his hair, and lowered herself carefully into the chair next to his, and had a sip of the coffee. "Heavens! This *is* dreadful." She put the cup down. "Amelia, would you mind awfully? There's got to be something potable with my name on it."

"Well, Mary and I were about to go—"

"Christ. Mary! I forgot all about Mary," my mother said. Harv threw his thick arm around her shoulder and pressed his chin to her forehead.

Then she turned to me. Her eyes were bright and hard to look at.

"Sit down, darling. There's something I want to tell you," she said.

My hands gripped the back of the chair. "I'm busy right now."

"This won't take long." She sat up taller, and pulled her robe tight about her neck. "Harv and I are going to spend a little time together. In California. That's what he came back to ask me, right? Isn't that right, Harv?"

"Sure is, sweetheart."

She drank again from his cup of coffee. There was something furtive about her then, like a mouse cornered by a cat.

"And until I get settled, you'll live with your father," she said.

"Are you *nuts?*" Shouting felt good, it felt strong.

"It's all arranged. I've already spoken to him. This morning, in fact. He's delighted to have you."

"I won't do it!"

My mother's face went still and flat, like when my father walked out the door with his suitcase.

"Mary will go back to her family, you'll spend time with your father, and that's that," she said.

Mary had seen this coming. That's why she'd been so weird with Harv. And then there she was, right beside me, drawn out by my shouts. She fixed my mother with such a firm stare that my mother looked away.

"She can't go back there," I said. "And you're *not* going to make her. You hear?"

"Hey, now, take it easy. No need to get all bent out of shape," said Harv.

"Shut up!"

"Amelia. You apologize to Harv this instant."

"The hell I will!"

Harv watched me. He started to look mean. Then my mother slumped, and massaged her forehead with her thumb.

"What's the matter, baby, you got a headache?" he asked her.

"Terrible."

"Aw, babe." He pulled her close. "You girls think you can bring this nice lady an aspirin or something?"

Mary stood still, her hands on her hips, and then she grabbed Harv's keys and was out the door. I was right behind her.

"Fuck that," she said.

"Totally fuck that."

She already had the engine on by the time I got in. The van was a trash heap. I tossed an old bag of French fries out the window, then wondered if maybe I shouldn't have, since we hadn't had any breakfast. We veered down the driveway and sideswiped my mother's peony bush.

"You ever drive before?" I asked.

"Not for a while. I just need to get the hang of it again, is all."

She gripped the wheel like an old woman and peered through the filthy windshield. When we reached the main road, she went so slowly that cars piled up behind and honked.

She sped up. We went around a wide bend, and when she didn't slow down enough for it, the tires squealed.

"Jesus!" I said.

"I'm okay. I got it now." We went on, into the gray-black sky. At the edge of town she went north, away from the lake and the willow-lined shore where we'd be spotted in no time. We didn't talk, because we were too busy trying not to think about what we were doing.

Then the rain broke loose. It splashed through the open windows, soaking us in no time. I leaned my head out the window and let it pelt my face. Mary turned onto a narrow country road, bordered by fields of grass. In the distance was an old barn, leaning badly, its roof in a sag. I imagined a snug, cozy house where you could live and not be bothered. When the rain stopped, the air shimmered, and the drops that held on the blades of grass were so lovely I didn't worry anymore.

AN IMAGINARY LIFE

Ted and Nina lie in bed and watch the moon rise over the desert like a single brilliant thought. He says she'd understand if she'd only try, and she puts her finger to his lips because in the world they have left behind—the rolling farmland of upstate New York—that same moon is shining on Lake Dunston and she's restless, in a mood to reminisce.

So she tells him a story.

About a Sunday afternoon in the late Sixties when she and her sister Ruth got stuck waiting outside a cocktail lounge at Newark Airport. Inside the lounge were her father and her Aunt Bip, drinking martinis. Bip was on her way back to Florida, and her flight was delayed. Ruth was sixteen, Nina was twelve.

Bip and Nina's father were talking about Ruth. Ruth was getting worse and plans had to be made. She couldn't return to the same school because she tried to seduce one of her teachers and then pulled the fire alarm when he turned down her invitation, and Bip knew of a place in Vermont that catered to "sensitive students."

"Bip?" says Ted.

"Short for Barbara Penelope."

"I'd have changed my name."

"To what?"

"An alias."

"A lie."

Ted shakes his head. "Always the straight shooter. Always the hard line." In the glow of the moon his face is so handsome. She runs her finger over the hard muscles of his arms. Her kisses are quick, then slow.

"Show me," she says.

"What?"

"The hard line."

He holds her close. After a minute he says, "You know I can't."

Nina turns away. "Then stop taking them, for Christ's sake!"

"We've talked about this."

"Maybe just go off them long enough for me to get laid."

"You'll get laid."

"When?"

"He told us. After a couple of months." *Loss of sexual interest is the most commonly cited side effect of anti-depressants.* Nina remembers little else of that visit except the doctor's white coat and the pattern in the yellow wallpaper behind him—some sort of abstract petals that looked like fingers or tongues.

"What if I quit you before then?" she asks.

"Then you won't get laid."

"Not by you." She looks at the wall.

"Hey, come on. Finish your story," he says.

"No."

"Come on. I want you to." The moonlight washes over them like an uneasy dream.

"Oh, all right."

Suddenly Ruth clutched Nina's arm. Three black men stood a few feet off, looking tired and dazed, wearing afros and dashikis, with three guitar cases on the floor. *The one on the end,* Ruth hissed. *That's Jimi Hendrix!*

Nina didn't believe her at first, but Ruth said no, she was sure because she'd just seen a picture of him in a magazine. She rushed up and asked Jimi for his autograph, and he dropped the pack of cigarettes he was holding, he was so surprised. He picked it up and stared down at them until Ruth asked him again. He found a piece of paper in one pocket, and a pen in another, and wrote *To Ruth, all my love forever, Jimi.*

"Do you still have it?" Ted asks.

"Oh, no. It got stolen. It was in her wallet, and someone lifted her purse."

"Bummer! What a story it would have made—Ruth the groupie, Ruth the underage lover, and with him dead and that piece of paper, who could prove you wrong?"

Nina leaves the bed and goes to the window, where the saguaro lift their arms to the silver sky.

"Nina, look, I—"

"It's okay."

"Come back to bed."

"In a minute."

Soon his breathing says he is asleep, and Nina remains by the window, remembering. Ruth wears a feather boa and races across their lawn. She sings an aria on the roof and her mother says, *Oh, for Heaven's sake, Nina, stop it! She's not crazy, she's just high-spirited.* Then Ruth calls from Vermont, where the snow falls even deeper than in Dunston, and whispers, *it's like being trapped, sometimes I dream I'm stuck in one and can't claw my way out.* Nina doesn't believe in ghosts, yet for a moment she is certain that Ruth is out there in the desert, trying to find her way home.

Two years before the desert, while the low September light drops into lake, Nina stops by the Dunston Market. In the produce section, a tall, attractive man in a tweed jacket stands with an orange in his hand. He considers it as if hoping it were something better, maybe a peach or an apple. He even lifts it up for a better look.

"Orange you going to buy it?" she asks. At thiry-four, her affairs have become routine, shabby episodes that end within a few months, and she sees nothing to lose.

Ted considers her blue cotton dress from the hem up before his eyes finds her face.

"Nothing rhymes with orange, you know," he says.

"I know."

"Smart girl."

"Orange thief." He's put the orange in his pocket by then, making a lopsided bulge.

"You like looking at a man below the belt, don't you?" he says, and she blushes the way she hasn't since grade school.

They go for drinks and talk. He's in the history department at the university, a junior colleague of her father's though he hasn't made the connection yet. She knew him right away. He had the attention of the whole room at the last cocktail party she went to with her father, a duty she performs to keep her father's social life alive since her mother seldom leaves home. Ted arranged the host's marble chess pieces to recreate the battle of Little Round Top during the Civil War, which he does again there in the bar restaurant using salted peanuts. The more he talks the more animated he becomes. His eyes shine, his finger tremble.

"And the officer in charge, Joshua Chamberlain, used an esoteric maneuver, sending his men down the mountain from the side, like a gate swinging closed, making the Confederates think they were outnumbered," he says. He stubs out his cigarette. "He was a college professor, thrust into a brand new life. A much more exciting one, I'd think."

"You sound jealous."

"Who wouldn't be? To escape one's life and the drudge of making a living."

"In exchange for getting shot at?" She's aware that she's smiling, her head slightly cocked.

Ted regards her. "You've heard this before, haven't you?" he asks.

"Yes, actually."

"You're a former student, making me look silly for not remembering you."

"I am a former student, you're right." Though his embarrassment is charming she lacks the heart to prolong it. "But not of yours, so don't worry." As she names her father, his damaged reputation shows in the lift of Ted's eyebrows—his heavy drinking, a severely depressed wife, the one daughter's possible suicide.

"He's a first-rate scholar," says Ted. That's true. Whatever else her father suffers, his research skills have not.

Ted offers her a cigarette. She declines. She tells a story of smoking as a teenager and setting her bedroom trash can on fire by mistake. She is home alone at the time and smothers the flames with a quilt her grandmother made years before. The quilt is burned through its center and to hide the flaw, Nina keeps it folded neatly on the end of her bed, with its good side always up. Later Ted says she's like that quilt, folded up tight, hiding her flaw and always showing her good side.

He makes it hard to. During their first year together he is often moody or sullen. She keeps him going with good cheer, passionate love, steady support. He can't get promoted, can't publish a good paper, can't stand teaching to students who live completely in the present. *Don't just memorize facts! Imagine what it was really like!* Then he embarks on a project he says will move him up the ladder. He works in his study until late at night, pen to paper, the computer unused. After weeks of being curious, asking what he's doing, Nina enters the study when he's not there. She finds a photo of a Confederate soldier bought for a dollar at an out-of-town flea market on their second date. And she finds something else, a leather journal full of Ted's handwriting. The first page says, *Private Diary of Joshua Himes, 25ᵗʰ Virginia Infantry.* The entries are dated during May and June, 1862. Joshua Himes is feisty, given to wild desires, inventive—there are several passages detailing an elaborate practical joke Himes plays on another soldier in camp, stealing personal articles like his straight razor and his pipe, then returning them by stealth until the soldier wonders about his own sanity. Himes talks about his superior officers, complains about pain in his teeth and right foot, describes the hard biscuits and tight jackets he must endure.

Nina has heard each story before. It's Ted, recalling his own time in military school after his father sent him there, then never called, never wrote, saying this would make a true man of him. Even the words are the same. When Joshua rebels against his own fictional father and challenges his poor opinion of him, he writes *I am one cocky son of God! I am filled with the purest wind!* That's what Ted shouted one summer night when he lifted Nina from the soft grass and twirled her until her hair flew.

Nina is stunned. *What are you thinking?* she asks more than once. *Were you going to pass this off as real? Don't you know how fast someone would see through it?*

He denies wanting anything of the kind. He says it's just a symptom of his own frustration, a necessary outlet. *The further I went, the more sense it made. And it was so easy to think my way into that place and time. Why can't you understand that, Nina? Why?* Because she doesn't like what's fake or pretend, and never will.

The Arizona morning is soft and clear. The heat that will rise later in the day is not yet felt on Nina's bare skin. This is the calming time. No diary, no memories of Ruth. She lifts her arms to the sky, then bends to touch her toes, and when she is upright once more a man stands across the road, watching her. The home behind him has been vacant, cars on the road are heard long before they're seen, which has made Nina feel secure in being there early each morning, naked.

Her body is not beautiful. It's long and bony, and her posture, always poor, gives her a slumped, lazy stance. Even so, her breasts are firm, and the muscles on her arms and legs are hard. She watches the man watch her and doesn't blush or turn away. He calls, "Good thing it's too early for the rattlers to be up and out!" He removes his cowboy hat before he speaks, and Nina is surprised to see a fine, thick head of iron-gray hair. She doesn't mean to smile, but she can't help being completely delighted at being found like that by a man she doesn't know, who is brave—or rude enough—to stand and grin right back. The embarrassment comes when she turns away, because she is particularly unhappy with the appearance of her small, boyish butt. The man's long, soft whistle sends a shiver down her knobby spine and at last she is blushing, and feeling warm, too, between her legs.

The toilet flushes down the hall, and Nina quickly puts on the robe she left on the kitchen counter. Ted appears, barefoot, in a T-shirt and shorts. He looks at the coffee maker which Nina turned on before going outside. She thinks again about the man across the road. She peeks slyly through the crack in the drapes. He's still there, taking things out of his pickup truck—boxes, a bag of golf clubs, a rocking chair.

Ted pours her a cup of coffee. The first sip burns her tongue.

"That story last night," he says.

"Yeah?"

"I've been wondering why it occurred to you."

"I don't know. I just think about her sometimes."

"Yeah, but why that particular story?" Nina brings the cup to her mouth, then remembers the burn and stops.

"Maybe because it was the last time Ruth and I did anything together. She left for school right after that."

Where she got even worse. Some days she refused to leave her bed, other days she'd leave the grounds at dawn, and roam around the little nearby town until someone went to bring her back. Or she'd be anxious, clingy, needing constant reassurance as she did that last day when she called home so much that Nina unplugged all the phones in the house. *Grow up*, Nina had thought. *Learn to deal with crap on your own.* Ruth's way of dealing was to sleep, so she took her pills and lost count of how many she'd taken. The family didn't learn of her death until two days after, when a police officer came to the door. *Something must be wrong with your phone*, he said. Nina had not put the lines back in their jacks, and her parents, always fairly reclusive, hadn't had to make a single call out.

"And then she died," says Ted.

"That first winter."

"Sucks."

Nina nods.

"Well, at least she got to meet Jimi Hendrix. Probably the highlight of her life," says Ted.

Ruth hadn't been quite as excited as Nina described. She'd held back, and Nina was the one to pull her forward.

Ted crosses the room and pulls open the curtain. The room explodes with light.

"Another sunny day," he says. "Imagine that." Ted hates the desert. Arizona was Nina's idea, on the theory that a complete change of scene would return him to the here and now. So might any of the activities she's introduced him to there, golf, cooking classes, a membership at a gym, biking, horseback riding, even hot-air ballooning. That was the worst. He held the rail in rigid silence and glared down at the receding ground as if it had no right to pull away like that. Nina had loved the freedom of drifting nearer the clouds, seeing their shadow lead them along like a wiser, silent version of themselves.

"You going to get that?" Ted asks when their phone rings. "You."

It's Nina's father, and Ted is glad to hear from him.

"You're kidding," Ted says into the receiver. "He *didn't* get tenure. Oh, that's too bad. Helps my chances though, doesn't it?"

At the window Nina watches her neighbor take a box out of his truck and carry it into the house.

"Great, we're doing great," says Ted says.

The story they told was that Nina wanted a break from Dunston for a while, maybe to find a new direction, and Ted would take the semester off, come along, and work on a book he was writing about Union troops in the Southwest after the Civil War, though he has yet to do any actual research.

"You sure can, hold on." Ted gives Nina the phone.

"How are you, Dad?" Nina asks.

"Old, Honey. Old." He sounds like his mouth is full of glue, which means he's on whiskey number three or four.

"How's Bip?"

"Fine. Bit fuzzy around the edges. Covers the same ground a little more than she used to. Remember the ring? Got that one twice last week."

"God."

Bip once had a lovely diamond solitaire—marquise-cut, one-and-a-half carats, a gift from her wealthy husband before he did nothing but drink. Her story was that she lost the ring in a card game, which was true, but not by a wager as one would assume. She'd removed the ring from her hand that was swelling from salted nuts, the Florida heat, and liquor. Later it couldn't be found, although the house was searched high and low, and Bip knew her hostess quietly relieved her of it while Bip assembled her full house.

"What about Mom?" Nina asks.

"Still at it. Going great guns, in fact." She's begun a series of paintings adapted from family photographs. One of Nina and Ruth, when Nina is ten, is in the works. From the ones already completed, Nina knows her mother will change the background from winter to summer, and give Ruth a smile she didn't show the camera, and while she knows there's a lot to be said for staying occupied, she can't see the point of taking one reality and then inventing another. The conversation ends as it always does, with her father saying she should just hang in there, that everything will settle down and be just fine.

"So, my old lady, she says to me, she says, 'Jud, you don't have it any more, and that's all I can say about that.'"

Nina's neighbor sits by her on his patio, which is just a square of unset bricks big enough for two folding chairs and a plastic cooler. They are shaded by a large umbrella wedged between two tires and held in place by elastic cords which pull in opposite directions, the way trunks of newly planted trees are kept upright. The cords are attached to two cinder blocks. It's an effective device, if not particularly pleasant to look at.

Jud is on his third beer. "She wasn't talking about sex, that's for damn sure."

"What, then?"

"Dunno. Whatever she needed to keep her in love, I guess." He belches softly. The lenses of his sunglasses are like mirrors, impossible to see behind, and Nina doesn't know if he's looking at her or the hills beyond her. It's over ninety in the shade, and yet Jud wears jeans and cowboy boots. His one concession to the heat is a bright white tee-shirt whose collar doesn't quite meet the leather string around his neck, and the four brilliantly blue turquoise stones it runs through.

"So, you folks liking it here?" asks Jud.

"I do, Ted doesn't."

"Not too friendly, is he, if you don't mind my saying."

Ted has refused Jud's invitations, rejected his overtures. *Jesus, Nina, the guy's got dipshit written all over him. Why can't he just leave us alone?*

"He retired or something?" asks Jud.

"On leave. He's a professor."

"Huh. What do you know about that."

The hem of Nina's sundress lifts in a lazy gust of wind, and fine grains of desert sand rise and drop away.

"Can I ask you something?" she says.

"Sure."

"You ever believe something that isn't true?"

"You mean a lie?"

"Something made up."

"Like Santa Claus?"

Nina laughs. Jud is so real, so down to earth. He's talked a lot about his days with the Arizona Border Patrol chasing "illegals," staking them out, and waiting, always waiting, for the next one to try his luck.

The beer she sips has warmed in the bottle from being held too long. She sets the bottle on the brick beside her chair and watches a hawk circle above the peak before her. The sun is so intense on the hillside that the saguaro seem to tremble.

"No, something you made up yourself. A fantasy. A dream. Maybe just a tall tale," says Nina.

"Not me, but I'll tell you about this guy I knew, Raoul." Jud takes a long drink of beer, puts the empty bottle on the ground, clasps his hands behind his head. "Now, this dude came over on the sly like so many do, then managed to stay, get a green card, a job, and eventually became a citizen. Worked for the Border Patrol as a translator. Most of the agents spoke decent Spanish, but once in a while some young guy would go on duty who didn't know a single word, which is where Raoul came in. At first all he did was explain the arrest process, a very one-way conversation. But then he got chatty and asked people questions, like where they were from, and what they were leaving behind, and then telling the agents all about it. Now, there's this one woman, a girl really, coming in all on her own with nothing but this little bag of stuff—a rosary, a picture of a man on a horse, and a comb, that's it. Well, Raoul takes himself a fancy to that old gal, and he tells the agent on duty, 'We have to help her, she's under threat of violence if she returns home to her village, some man wants to marry her and says he'll have her whether they make it legal or not.'

"So, the agent, this big dumb guy name of Clyde gets a soft spot and says okay, he'll see what he can do with the INS, maybe go to bat for her. And Raoul takes charge, finds her a place to live, gets her a job as a maid in Scottsdale, where the signora happens to speak lovely Spanish and quickly finds out that her Guadalupe wasn't fleeing anything of the kind, at least not the way Raoul described it. She was just looking for a better life, like they all are."

"Why did he lie?" Nina asks.

"He didn't really lie, he just stretched the truth a little. Yeah, there was a guy who had his eye on her back home, but there was nothing improper about it. Raoul was a romantic, is all. Likes to give everyone his own bit of drama. Made up tales about quite a few of them, I understand. Didn't get him in as much trouble as you might think, a reprimand, and an unpaid vacation. Spent it back home in Juarez, and you know what? He stayed."

Again, Nina laughs. He's very charming. He's never

mentioned seeing her naked that morning three weeks ago, and she's never raised it, either. It's there all the same, like his interest, which fueled by a little beer, makes him lean in and kiss her lightly on the cheek.

"You can slap me now," he says.

"I'm not the slapping kind."

"You the kissing kind?"

"Maybe. If the time is right."

The heat, the beer, and her bold words make her feel like a balloon that's rising away, out of sight.

"I'm sorry, I shouldn't have said that," she said.

"Hey, I kissed you and I'm not sorry."

"I have to go."

"Okay."

She stands, and gives him her empty bottle. She's reflected in his sunglasses—two tiny blushing Ninas.

"Come back anytime," he says.

"I will."

She makes her way across the road in the blinding glare, then in the shade of the corrugated roof that shields the walk she passes the trash can. Ted has left the lid off again. She picks up the lid, and as she lowers it to the can she sees Ted's forged diary in the remains of last night's pasta salad.

Inside the house the cool air is startling. Ted is asleep on the couch, the television showing another soap opera. *Tell me the truth, Jason, for the love of God* a miserable old woman pleads to a much younger man. Nina turns off the television set. She sits and recalls Ted's quiet, anguished voice, *I just needed to write it, that's all.*

So he could walk out of his life and get a breath of fresh air. Now he has returned to himself and let go of Joshua Himes. How odd that it had happened while she was out drinking with Jud. Well, maybe not so odd.

She studies his face. It's calm, peaceful, the jaw line softer with the weight he gained when he quit smoking. He did that for her, at her insistence. And he came to Arizona because she thought was that was the right thing to do, too.

His eyes open slowly, and their light is clear. "Hey," he says.

"Hey."

"What time is it?"

"I don't know. A little after four."

He stretches. "Jesus, I had the weirdest dream."

"What about?"

"An orange. Or maybe a peach." He sits up and scratches his chin. She gets herself a glass of water in the kitchen, drinks it, and pats water on her face with a dishtowel.

"Hotter than hell out there," she says.

"What else is new?"

This time of year the breezes off of Lake Dunston are barely warm. The willows on the shore sway and rustle, as if to music only they can hear.

"You know what I'm thinking?" Nina asks.

"I never know what you're thinking."

"About going home."

Ted stares at her. "And leave your new buddy? He'll be crushed."

"Bull. I'm not his type. He likes Hispanic women. He's got one over in Globe, in fact."

Ted shuffles the deck he keeps on the coffee table, not well because he doesn't know how, and several cards drop to the floor.

"Let me do that," says Nina and joins him on the couch. She picks up a fallen card. "King of hearts," she says, and kisses his cheek. She collects all the cards, takes a group in each hand, and shuffles them together quickly and expertly.

He asks where she learned how to do that, and she says she once had a boyfriend who worked as a dealer at an Indian casino near Dunston.

"Is that true?" he asks.

She smiles and gives him the cards to lay out a new game.

"Forget solitaire, let's play poker," he says.

"I don't know how."

"I'll show you. The rules are easy. It's the psychology that's tough."

"As in having a 'poker face?'"

"Right. Just keep your cool, build your hand, and don't show it until you have to."

In a year, or five, or ten, they might mention the diary and say it was Ted's flight of fancy, an expression of true creative genius, or they might call it something else they can't imagine now.

Because when he declared those things to her under the stars above the lake, he didn't know that Joshua would one day write them in his diary. And the day she saw Jimi Hendrix at the airport, Nina didn't know that she would later say Ruth saw him first and then begged for the autograph when Nina did both, because Ruth died alone, unable to reach home, and Nina didn't.

That autograph still lies in her jewelry box, under her bracelets and chains. *To Nina, all my love forever, Jimi.*

SNOW ANGELS

At first it was nothing. Then it fell harder, and
they had to slow down. Cory had never liked
snow, even from inside a warm place. As a child
she thought it sucked color from the world, a comment
that made her family laugh. For a few years now they'd
circled her left ankle—balloon heads and dots for eyes—
and when she pointed her toe their faces became thin and
scant. Too bad she couldn't do that to them in real life, she
always thought.

In the back seat Vic was sleeping off his airplane drinks.
At six-four Vic had to curl up tight to fit in Lander's car.
Lander was Cory's brother, and she hadn't told him Vic
was coming. When he met them at the terminal, Lander
observed Vic's leather coat and shaved head and asked,
without offering his hand, "How do you do?"

"Super, man, and you?"

Lander hadn't said another word to Vic since.

From Newark Airport to Dunston was usually three
hours, and now the weather would make it over four. Just
then they were in the wilds of eastern Pennsylvania.

"You didn't have to come all the way down for me,"
Cory told Lander.

"Just wanted to make sure you'd make the final leg okay."

"Afraid I'd change my mind? Bail out at the last minute?"

"It had occurred to me."

Their father was dying. He'd been dying a long time, a slow progression of some blood disorder Cory didn't remember the name of. There had been several false alarms, and then a slight recovery after each transfusion. Now there was no recovery, only the certainty that options had been exhausted and the time had come to gather.

Vic snored. Lander lowered the window above Vic's head, and the snow blew in on him. Cory pressed the button on her arm-rest and raised the window.

"You're an asshole," she said.

"Where did you get this guy, anyway?"

"Met him on the plane."

"Jesus Christ!"

"I'm kidding."

Vic had come into the tattoo parlor one day and stayed. That was eight months ago. Since then he'd learned how to ink almost as well as Cory did. He'd done her latest, an arrow embedded in the tight skin above her heart, the place closed up and both of them naked, downing shots of tequila, sucking on limes, sucking on each other, the buzzing pen steady no matter how much booze or sex she gave him. In spite of that, Vic was really pretty tame. Once, tame would have been a quick ticket out the door, but now, at twenty-eight, tame had taken on some charm. *Can't go on all my life getting bounced off the walls,* Cory had told him. That was as strong a statement of love as she'd ever made.

The snow fell harder. Every few minutes Lander sucked his teeth, a habit from childhood that meant despite the absolute stillness of his face, he was terrified. After living all his life in snow country it still rattled him. Served him right for not getting out, the way she had.

Sometimes, when he thought to call—which he hadn't

done for almost two years before last week's summons—he asked when she planned to move back there. As if her going wasn't permanent. As if, given the small group of people related to her, she'd ever consent to live in the Finger Lakes again, or anywhere in New York state, or the entire east coast, for that matter.

She lit a cigarette. Lander rolled his eyes. He disapproved of smoking, along with laziness, tardiness, or slackness of any kind. He held his language arts students to the highest standards of performance, so much so that he'd been told twice by the principal to "lighten up a little." His own wife had left him two years before for having, as she put it, "a rod up his ass."

"I need it. Don't lecture me about secondhand smoke, either," Cory said, and blew smoke his way on purpose. Lander sighed and sounded just like their father who sighed a lot, brief huffs when he was angry, and a longer, more leisurely release of air when he wanted to express disappointment. To Cory he had expressed a great deal of disappointment over the years for not being a good student like Lander, for having the wrong sort of boyfriend—motorcycle riders, dropouts, even an ex-con—a general lack of sympathy with the human race and its finer points, but most of all because she was completely uninterested in the achievements that had earned him grants, promotion to full professor at Dunston University at a relatively young age, and later the position of chairman of the English Department. He had never said so flat out, but she knew this was his major grief with her—that she refused to be impressed.

Paula had been impressed enough for everyone. *How can you act like that, Cory? Think of your father's reputation! He's a very well-respected man, you know.*

Paula was her father's second wife. The first wife, Cory and Lander's mother, died when Cory was five and Lander seven. Cory remembered a gray and green funeral parlor.

Summer light fought its way through stained glass windows. *It's like a kaleidoscope,* Cory whispered and was pinched hard. Then an urn was put in her father's hands. It sat in his closet in the old house, and came into the house he bought with Paula. Paula wanted it gone. Cory's father threw the ashes in Lake Dunston one winter day, his children shivering and whining from the cold.

Vic coughed again, stretched, and sat up. "Oh, man, look at that snow!" he said.

"That's what it is," said Cory.

"It's awesome."

Lander looked at Cory.

"Grew up in Pasadena. Not used to it," she said.

"Pasadena. Really," said Lander.

"Yup. Nothing but sunshine and blue sky. Some say it's paradise. I say it sucks," said Vic.

"Indeed."

Lander left the highway for a smaller state road that would twist and turn them into Dunston in another hour. The snow went on falling. Lander took some peanut butter crackers from the box he'd stuffed by his seat—cheaper than stopping for dinner. Cory fed herself and Vic on two stale bagels and four little bottles of scotch she'd bought on the plane.

Her father used to be quite the scotch drinker, himself, every afternoon, home from campus, in his black easy chair, a glass in hand while the household revolved around him. Paula asking what he'd like for dinner, her daughter Debbie needing a kiss on her chubby cheek, Lander quiet and watchful, and Cory pushing past them all. *I came in third in the spelling bee, Daddy. Missed 'philanthropy.' You know my friend, Melissa, her dad teaches, too, some science or other, anyway, she said I did really great.* To that her father gave a quick nod. At thirteen she had the word "kindness" tattooed on the inside of her wrist.

Can't you understand it's permanent? her father said. *A thing you can never take back?* Like certain words, she thought later, remembering how he'd called her a "fool," and then when she was older a "slut."

"This was a bad idea," Cory said.

"What is?"

"My coming here."

"He *asked* for you. How many times must I say it?"

The snow drove straight into the headlights. Cory stared at the bright rushing mix and tried over and over to follow the path of a single flake. It was impossible.

"So, when do I see him?" she asked.

"Tomorrow, first thing."

"Fine."

A car ahead skidded, its red taillights making a zigzag in the dark.

"Do you have something decent to wear?" Lander asked.

"Meaning what?"

"A turtleneck."

A vine of ivy was inked across the skin of Cory's throat.

"You don't think he'll appreciate the joke?" she asked. Lander's eyebrows came together.

"As in Ivy League," she said.

"Aren't you clever."

"Sure am."

"And perhaps childish." On the phone she'd said it would serve her father right if she didn't come at all, that he was probably lying when he said he wanted to see her. When Lander tried to interrupt, she said, *Fuck him.* "And resentful. To the point of being unpleasant. Even a bitch, at times."

"Hey, Lander. It's Lander, right?" Vic asked.

"Yes?"

"Now, I'm not a gambling sort of guy, never was, to be honest, but I still bet you the lousy fifty bucks I got in my pocket that there's no need, whatsoever, for that kind of talk."

Lander stared at Vic for a moment in the review mirror. Vic smiled at him and shrugged.

Cory could tell Vic things about Lander that would drop his opinion even lower. The question was whether those things were past or present tense. She pulled down her visor, leaned into the mirror as if to check her teeth, and looked back at Vic to make sure he was still staring out the window. She put the visor back, then she slipped her hand inside the neck of her sweater—a man's cashmere she'd bought at a thrift shop—and exposed the soft skin just above her left breast.

Lander peered down her front and pretended not to. He did it quickly, with a fast, practiced drop of the eyes. He'd done a lot of looking at her that he'd tried to hide. She'd used it growing up, a power she had over him. *Tell me this and I'll show you that.* What she'd wanted to know was always about their father, what he'd said about her, what he'd do next where she was concerned. What she got for her trouble were things like *he loves me better* and *he says I'm a lot smarter than you*, pain she left on the bodies she marked for life, and in the ears of young men who shared her bed before Vic came along. One of them, whose name might have been Brian or Brad, had said of Lander's foibles, *Hey, it takes two to tango, you know.*

Dunston came into view. The family house the same, the bushes crushed by snow. Paula's daughter, Debbie, at the door, little changed, still childlike with her small, sullen mouth. Paula in the kitchen, her bony fingers like claws around her glass, her eyes sunken in her once beautiful face. She and Lander embraced. Then Paula turned to Cory and Vic and looked at them as if they were mist or smoke, something temporary and inclined to form a lazy, useless swirl.

"How is he today?" Lander asked Paula.

"Same. Quiet. Wants to see you. Both of you. Especially Cory."

"I bet," said Cory.

Paula stared up into Vic's face. "I can make up the couch for you. It's not very comfortable, but I'll do my best."

"He stays with me," said Cory.

"Oh. Well. Of course. Only, I don't know what your poor father would think."

"He'd think I'm an adult."

Paula nodded. Her face was pinched. She was crying, Cory realized. She'd never, in her entire life, seen Paula cry.

The bed they slept in that night was her old one, in a different place now, a spare room off her father's first floor study. The same bed she and Lander had woken up in together years before, naked, hung over, neither knowing then or later if they'd committed an act of incest. Debbie discovered them. Paula and their father were out of town, at a conference in New York City, and Lander and Cory were given this one chance to prove their responsibility as teenagers and keep an eye on their ten-year-old charge, the house, and the crabby, arthritic dog who needed to be helped down the front stairs several times a day to piss and shit in the yard. What they did was raid the liquor cabinet, send Debbie to bed, and forget about the dog, who made a mess all over Paula's Persian rugs. They played a game of strip poker, which Cory lost, leaving her to sit shivering and naked before Lander who wouldn't let her dress. She challenged him to shots of whiskey to see who could drink the most and still function. After that she remembered nothing except Debbie shoving her awake to say the dog needed to go out. Lander and Cory both bribed her to keep quiet, not about their night together, which they denied even to themselves, but about the rest of it. She didn't. She went straight to Paula and blabbed the whole story, mad that she'd been exiled to her room when they'd promised they'd all stay up and watch late night movies with popcorn. Their father assumed it was Cory's doing, that she'd lured her brother into bed and God alone knew what else, and it was then she who was exiled. The school in Vermont she attended for her last two years of high school was expensive, almost beyond his means, but he made the sacrifice for the sake— and salvation—of his son, Lander. Cory never went home after that, but fled to L.A. and built a world out of booze, sex, and her beloved tattoos.

Paula was talking to Cory slowly, as if from a dream, one hand to her hair, her throat, and back again, a sleepwalker recalling a gracious gesture, perhaps on entering a room where the faces were turned her way and the smiles all meant for her.

Lander was pushing for hospice care, she said, thinking it was better to bring him home. The trouble was, he didn't want to come home, didn't want to be a burden to anyone, wanted everyone to carry on without him and get used to his being gone. Debbie, beside her mother on the waiting room's vinyl couch, told Cory that she too had urged Cory's father in this direction, with no luck. Paula asked Cory what could be taking so long, and Debbie told Cory it was probably nothing important, another sponge bath, or changing the sheets. Talking through her was new, Cory thought. Once they spoke around her, ignoring her altogether, sometimes referring to her in the third person. *She thinks you don't know who got into your wallet,* and *Go on, honey, tell me what she did this time,* Cory sometimes occupying the physical space between them and once grabbing both mother and daughter by the arm and screaming, *I'm not fucking invisible, you assholes!* She was no more visible now, really, only necessary to keep in place the distance they seemed to need, for reasons she didn't want to know.

Lander appeared in the hallway leading from their father's room. He walked rigidly, as if his back gave him an agony.

"He wants to see Cory. Alone," he said.

"Why?" Cory asked.

"How should I know? I'm just the messenger."

"You want I should hang out, or what?" Vic asked Cory. Debbie look startled at the sound of his voice, as if she'd already forgotten his existence. She went on working with whatever was in her hands, knitting, from the look of it.

"If you want. I don't know how long I'll be," said Cory.

"Fine with me."

Suddenly, Cory was terrified. She collected her scarf and coat and went alone down the hall. He lay by the window. He was the same, only pared down. Skin like paper, skull clearly outlined, the fingernails translucent half-moons.

At the sound of her steps he opened his eyes slowly. They were unfocused for a moment, then settled sharply on her.

"Corrine. Well." His voice was faint, yet not weak, as if he could still get the attention of the whole room if he wished to. His eyes traveled to her cropped green hair, her face, and her bare arms revealed by a sleeveless blouse she'd worn to show off the garden that trailed from bicep to wrist. "You're quite the sight."

He didn't seem to expect any sort of embrace, or gesture of affection, and she made none. She sat down, her crumpled wool coat—another thrift-store find—on her lap. He gestured to her to press the button which raised the top half of the bed, allowing him to sit up taller.

"What are they?" he asked. He meant her tattoos.

"Lilies here, and this is a rose, and on this side a daisy chain."

"Very lifelike. Your designs?"

"Yes."

"Well."

His eyes closed, he exhaled slowly. *He's in pain*, she thought. *A shitload of pain.* No one had prepared her for that. They were probably all used to it by now, since they converged on him daily according to Lander, but still someone should have told her. That wasn't how they did things, though. They'd always expected her to fend for herself.

She waited for him to continue, and he didn't. Her gaze wandered. The window gave a wide view of the hills sloping down to Lake Dunston—a view so lovely Cory wondered how Paula had managed to arrange it, unless Debbie had. Debbie was absurdly devoted to Cory's father, principally because he'd funded a lot of her nonsense, like taking a spiritual tour of India, living in an ashram for several months, then coming back to Dunston and doing absolutely nothing except toy with the notion of one day getting a career, perhaps as a social worker. The snow resumed, and slowly the view was obscured. Cory shivered, although the room was too warm.

She needed a cigarette.

"I'll be right back," she said.

His hand found her wrist and held on with surprising strength.

"No," he said.

"Just a quick cigarette break. It's all right."

"No. You *must* stay here. I need to speak to you."

So, she sat. Lunch was brought. Her father waved it away, and famished, Cory helped herself. Rubbery slices of pale turkey, a flawless mound of mashed potatoes in which a small depression was filled with gummy and delicious gravy. The green beans were cold and chewy, but she ate those, too, and the small square of apple turnover that served as dessert. She looked inside her purse, hoping the extra serving of whiskey she'd gotten on the plane was still there, and it was. She opened the tiny bottle, and drank it quickly.

"Your mother—" her father said. He sighed, cleared his throat, swallowed with difficulty, and continued. He wasn't able to properly express his affection towards her; he'd lived in fear that he would always disappoint her, not live up to her as an equal—she was a brilliant woman in her own right, did Cory know that? Not academically, but in the way she saw inside people, understood them quickly and completely. It scared him. Sensing his withdrawal, she, too withdrew and grew cold, long before she died.

Paula was entirely different, he said. She was dense, oblivious, in her own world, yet she always held him in the highest esteem. It meant total freedom. When you can do no wrong, he explained, then you are at liberty to do anything you please. And he did. Money he shouldn't have spent; insulting comments about Paula's cooking while she presided over their table with grace; affairs with students he kept quiet except for one that went too far, the student calling the house, banging on the door, tracking them down in restaurants. He denied it to Paula, said the girl was disturbed, obsessed, completely deranged, which a subsequent suicide attempt confirmed. Paula believed him.

"Maybe she just pretended to," said Cory.

"Same result. I was off the hook."

He spoke next of Debbie, her inability to get traction in life, a fundamental laziness that prevented her from evolving. Her mother had left her emotionally isolated, and she'd turned to Cory's father for support, for love she had to have. He couldn't give it to her. She was sweet in her way, and he was fond of her, yet found he couldn't love her. That was his defect as a person, he supposed, and something he was powerless to change.

A nurse appeared to record some numbers from one of the monitors connected to Cory's father by plastic tubing.

Cory felt the liquor now, and wished she had more. The nurse was tall and stocky with thick arms, a no-nonsense gal with a heart of gold.

"You doing okay?" she asked Cory. Cory knew she smelled of whiskey. The old sense of exposure, of being found out.

"Fine, thank you." Up straighter in her seat. One hand gliding through her emerald hair to keep it smooth. "But I think he might need something," she said.

Nurse Huge turned his way. "Mr. Giles? Can I bring you anything?"

A head feebly shaken. A sympathetic glance exchanged between the women in the room.

The nurse then bent down to Cory and whispered, "You're all he needs, all he's asked for these last weeks, God bless you for being here, for coming such a long way."

"Further than you know." But she was gone, that good nurse, on to some other sufferer, and Cory was sure she hadn't heard.

"What?"

"Nothing, Dad. Just talking to myself."

"You used to."

"No. You're thinking of Lander."

Alone in his room, his voice stopping, then starting over, as if rehearsing a part in a play, only the play was his own life, *she is pretty, yes, oh, she is pretty, is she as pretty as the one who got sick and died, do you mean your mother, I mean nothing, oh, then nothing makes you mean,* his wordplay brilliant, scary, tragic.

"He's—unbalanced," her father said, then added that Lander had tried all his life to regiment things to cover his own foibles. He was rigid, uncompromising, lived in a little box because it was safe. His mind was reliable enough, but his spirit was wild, destructive, untrustworthy. He was as hard as stone, yet without the slightest degree of self-control.

What about me? Cory wondered. She'd been a madwoman herself. Bouncing from passion to passion, full of nothing but bitter dust. She came back to Dunston only for revenge, she realized, to sit by her dying father and remind him of all the hurt she'd suffered. He was the one suffering, though. Who had suffered, perhaps as much as she.

"He always admired you in a way I found—disturbing," her father said.

Cory crushed her scarf in both hands. "Well, he—"

"It became dangerous as you grew older. I'd hoped nothing would come of it, but I was wrong."

Cory released her scarf. The liquor was stale in her mouth.

"So I sent you away." He swallowed. "I saw the harm that might come to you otherwise."

It is necessary for me to separate you from your brother, and that's the only explanation I will make. She'd begged to stay, not wanting to leave her few friends and oddly enough, even Lander. Lander might have known her father's mind. His letters to her were overly kind. *Everyone misses you, even Debbie, though she's too snotty to say so.* The kindness faded in time, replaced with neutral updates on the family, and later, as she responded by detailing the seediness of her life, contempt.

Her father's eyes closed once more, and his chin sank to his chest. Soon his breathing was deep and slow. Cory rose, and made her way through the hall with her coat already on, down the elevator, through the sliding doors, and into the cold. The flakes were fat now, meaning the storm was nearly done. A nurse sat on a bench, wrapped in a parka, smoking. She nodded at Cory, and Cory nodded back. Cory found her own cigarettes, lit one, and went on standing in the spinning snow. She stuck out her tongue, let a flake land there and melt.

Lander came through the door, walking his crooked gait.

"What are you doing out here?" he asked.

She lifted her cigarette. He dug his hands into his lower back, then twisted side to side.

"What did you do to yourself?" Cory asked.

"Shoveled too much snow."

"Jesus."

They reminisced about the time their father had a similar injury, how he roared and bellowed and ordered everyone out of his way, then demanded ice packs and a stiff drink.

Vic came through the door next, his magazine rolled up under his arm.

"Why didn't you come and get me?" he asked Cory.

"I just had to get outside."

"I know. But I can't give moral support if I'm sitting in there on my ass."

"Sorry."

He flapped his arms. He was probably freezing and didn't say so. Cory liked that about him.

Then Lander turned to Vic and said, "I'd like to talk to Cory."

"So, talk." Vic stayed put. That morning after breakfast Cory heard Lander and Vic in the kitchen. Vic said he thought the house was great, he'd had no idea that Cory had grown up in such a place, that he himself had lived in a trailer park after his father went to jail, and Lander said he hoped Vic wasn't getting any ideas about a big inheritance Cory might be in for, at which point Vic asked if Lander would like to get his ass kicked, free of charge.

"It's okay. It'll just be a minute. Go back and get warm," said Cory.

"Nah." Vic moved off, picked up some snow, packed into a hard ball and pitched it out over the lawn of the hospital. He turned back and grinned.

Lander watched Vic throw more snowballs. Then he looked at Cory with their father's same eyes, only deeper, and more intense.

"So, how did it go? Did he say anything important?" he asked.

"Not really."

"You sure?"

"Of course I'm sure."

Even when they were kids, Lander had had keen radar. *Why do you look like that, Cory? Isn't there something you want to tell me?* And there usually was. *I spit on Debbie while she was sleeping. I stole Paula's pin and threw it in the woods.*

"No hidden fortunes? No confessions about how one of us was really adopted? No last-minute revisions to his will?" Lander never did well, trying to be funny.

Even from about twenty feet away Cory heard Vic's cell phone sing out a cheerful up-and-down tune from the depths of his coat pocket. He took it out and looked at the screen.

"Bernie," he called to her. "Think I should take it?"

"Sure. See what that fat fuck wants now."

Bernie was their sometimes roommate. When his wife got sick of him, which she did every few months, they gave him their spare room in exchange for a couple of hundred dollars. At the moment he was house-sitting for them. House-sitting amounted to watering the two ferns, putting the mail where they could find it again, and making the place look occupied so no one broke in.

Lander was still looking at Cory, willing her to speak. *The harm that might come to you, otherwise.*

"What is it?" Lander asked.

"Nothing. I just feel—"

"Yes?"

"Stupid."

"He always makes you feel that way."

Her gaze settled on a tree in the near distance, its branches all white and fluffy. A gust of wind sent flakes and ice crystals around their heads. All of a sudden she remembered sledding out on the old golf course.

Vic returned. "He wanted to know if he could rent a movie on our account at the video place." Cory looked at him. "No, not porn. Documentary on Africa, if you can believe that." He blew on his hands, which were pink from the snowballs. He looked at Cory, then at Lander, then at Cory again.

"You know how to make snow angels?" he asked.

"What?"

"Isn't that what kids do around here? Make snow angels?"

The back yard full of them, Cory and Lander back inside just long enough to get warm, then out again to make more.

"I guess," said Cory.

"Show me."

"Go on, I should get back," said Lander.

Cory watched Lander go, his head down, hands shoved deep in his pockets.

"Come on. Show me!" Vic said again. He threw a snowball at her. She ducked. She led him onto the lawn, lay down on her back, and swung her legs and arms up and down. The snow was refreshing. It had stopped falling, she realized.

"Cool!" said Vic. He plopped down, made one of his own, then lay laughing at himself. He got to his feet and brushed himself off. Then he pulled her up and brushed her.

"You know, it's fucking freezing out here. What say we go in and get a cup of rotgut coffee?" he asked.

Arm in arm they walked. Vic shivered. "Fuck. Got some in my boots."

"That's the problem with snow."

"Still, it makes everything pretty, don't you think?"

All around them the new snowfall took on a silver light under the weak sun, but then as the clouds moved southward into the valley and opened the sky above the hills, it became pure white, absolutely clear, and almost too beautiful to bear.

The Comforts of Home

In the Finger Lakes town of Dunston, New York, the spring rain had fallen for four straight days, and was falling again when the old man moved in. He carried one box at a time from the trunk of his Cadillac while Beau stood across the street and watched. He wondered what it would be like having an old man in the trailer park. Everyone else was younger. Beau and his wife, Eldeen, were in their twenties. The people next to them were about the same age, with four kids who slept in bunk beds in their living room. On the other side of them was a gay guy who worked at Target, and next to him was a retired cop. No one was friendly or even nice, something Eldeen often complained about.

The old man was careful as he hauled his boxes inside. Beau had seen old men like that in Iraq, setting out their fruit in the market, their veined hands slow and sure. The younger men's hands were fast and reached his way to greet or beg, or sometimes were hidden deep in the pockets of their Western pants, which made him go quiet and cold wondering what they'd pull out.

Beau wished he had his old slingshot. Even a small rock would make a big noise on the metal siding of the old man's trailer. The old man might hit the deck, thinking he was being shot at. That would be something to see.

The old man hauled another box to the trailer, and stumbled on the top stair. Beau laughed. He couldn't help it. He'd always found that kind of thing funny. Once, Eldeen stumbled and he laughed for about five minutes. She didn't talk to him then for three whole days.

The old man appeared in the doorway, stared down at his car as if he'd forgotten what he was doing, and went back inside. Beau wondered if he were loopy. His own grandfather had lost his marbles in his early seventies and imagined a whole family of people who'd never existed. Eldeen said he couldn't have suffered from Alzheimer's in that case, because if he did, he'd have forgotten people, not made them up. Eldeen thought she knew what she was talking about because of her leg. Suffering might give you wisdom, Beau thought, but then again, it might not.

Eldeen drove up in their pickup truck. She was a pretty woman, with wavy brown hair she liked to put clips in. Today they were shaped like strawberries. She'd had to go to the grocery store and he didn't want to go along. Grocery shopping was the most boring thing he'd ever done. Eldeen didn't mind it. She went up and down the aisles talking to herself, commenting on the prices of things, wondering aloud if she should make this or that for dinner. He used to tell her not to, because people looked at her.

"They look at me anyway," she said, again because of her leg. Sometimes she used a crutch with a brace that went around her upper arm. It caused a sore just above the elbow, so she only used it when she had to.

Eldeen got out of the truck.

"Who's that?" she asked Beau.

"Beats me."

"Must be a new neighbor."

"Must be."

Eldeen limped across the road. It was a fairly wide road, and it took her a little time. When she reached the old man's car, he came down the stairs and shook Eldeen's hand. Eldeen ran her fingers through her hair, something she did when she was nervous, then pointed behind her. *That's us, just across there,* Beau imagined her saying. *Oh, yes, it's a nice little place here, isn't it?* Eldeen was upbeat. A little too upbeat at times. The old man lifted his arm toward his open door, and they both went inside. She didn't come out for several minutes. *Why, if this isn't the cutest old place you have here! Folks that lived here before weren't too neighborly.* Eldeen had tried to make friends with them, too. She and the wife had had words in the end, about what Beau didn't know. Eldeen appeared in the door of the old man's trailer, then limped down the three concrete steps that all the trailers in the park had, across the road, and up the stairs to her own home.

Beau brought in the groceries from the truck. At the store someone else loaded them for her, and then Beau was always home to bring them inside. Beau had been discharged from the Army for over six months and still hadn't found work. He spent a lot of time eating cereal and watching the news. Eldeen kept the books for a liquor store three days a week. They'd asked her to go full-time. She didn't care to, but would if need be. "And you know what *that* means," she said. She threatened to turn all household chores over to him. Beau hadn't handled a broom, vacuum cleaner, or dirty dish since he returned. Before he enlisted, he helped out a lot, even though he had a full-time job then as a cashier at the drug store.

With the recession the only place hiring was the gun factory, and Beau didn't want to think about guns. A guy he'd gotten close to in Iraq shot himself in the head one night after another guy they sometimes played cards with got blown up in a roadside bombing. Beau had tried to wrench the gun free from the dead guy's hand, and couldn't. He didn't remember trying to remove the gun. The whole thing was a blank. Someone else had told him what he'd done. He'd tried to put it together, make sense of his action, and couldn't. "Maybe you were only trying to help him. Maybe you didn't know he was already gone," Eldeen said. Beau thought it was possible. His uncle, the one who lost his mind in Vietnam, sat around his parents' basement and played Russian Roulette with his sidearm. One day the uncle was passed out drunk, and Beau took the gun and threw it in the creek. He wasn't accused of taking it because everyone knew the uncle wasn't right in the head. It was said that he had hocked it, or locked it up some place he couldn't remember. Eldeen kept a nine-millimeter in the drawer of her bedside table. "In case we get robbed," she'd said. Beau thought she was nuts. For one thing, she didn't know how to use it. For another, they didn't have anything someone would risk getting shot at to come in and steal. He'd like to get rid of that gun, too, and knew he'd have to explain himself to Eldeen. So, the gun stayed put.

Summer came, and everyone's windows opened. The trailers were in a tight cul-de-sac and sounds normally kept inside leaked out. From the cop's place came classic rock. The big family had Disney tunes. The Target guy, when he was home, liked opera. Only the old man kept quiet. Beau was charged with keeping the grass cut along the common strip, and once, as he pushed his mower, he leaned in close under the old man's kitchen window and heard a talk radio program discussing the pros and cons of uniform health coverage.

One evening Eldeen and Beau sat on their stairs and watched the twilight fall. He took her hand in his, and after a moment she took it back and ran it through her hair.

"Guess what?" she asked.

"Can't."

"I asked Sam if you could drive their delivery truck." Sam was Eldeen's boss at the liquor store.

"I don't want to drive a truck."

"He said he'd see what he could do."

"I don't need his charity."

"It's not charity if he's paying you."

Her eyes were different, he thought. They had a quiet, private look to them that wasn't there before.

Beau kissed her neck. "You worry too much. Everything will be fine."

The old man came walking down the road. He had on khaki pants and a pressed shirt. He saw Eldeen and Beau and made his way over to them. Eldeen smiled. The old man held out his hand to Beau.

"Clifford Benderhoff," he said. Beau shook his hand.

"Beau," he said.

"Lovely night."

"Yeah."

"Just out taking my constitutional."

"Right."

Mr. Benderhoff shifted his focus from Beau to Eldeen. "Well, good night," he said.

"Good night," said Eldeen.

Mr. Benderhoff went briskly across to his own trailer.

"He talks like a professor, doesn't he?" asked Eldeen.

"If you say so."

"He used to teach college, you know. He told me so that first day."

Beau snorted. Someone was pulling Eldeen's good leg. No one who used to teach college would end up living in a trailer. Beau didn't know why the old man would say such a thing to her, and figured he might be a little loopy, after all.

After that Eldeen looked out for Mr. Benderhoff. She brought him bland casseroles and cheese bakes, stuff Beau couldn't imagine a guy with no teeth would manage, given how hard and chewy everything Eldeen made was.

"What makes you think he has no teeth?" Eldeen asked.

She was at the sink in a sleeveless top with a little lace collar that made her look cute.

"So, he's got teeth. How come you gotta feed him all the time?"

"Hon. It was last Tuesday, Thursday, and today."

Beau scratched his chin. He was growing a beard. Eldeen said once that she liked beards.

"Where's his family to feed him?" he asked.

"Widower. Daughter all the way out in California."

"He should move out there. Old people need lots of sunshine."

"He's not that old. Just seventy-two."

"That's pretty old, if you ask me."

Her expression said she wasn't asking him, and wouldn't.

The first time Eldeen visited Mr. Benderhoff, he said she should call him Cliff, short for Clifford. He invited her to sit in a chair by the living room window. Nearby two other chairs were wrapped in old blankets. Boxes were stacked against the far wall, and a robust ivy plant sat on the kitchen table and trailed down to the floor. Cliff saw where she was looking and explained that he'd had the plant for many years and had taken it with him every time he moved. She asked why he moved so often, and the slow wandering of his clear blue eyes, as if he were struggling to make sense of his new home, said he was lonely. Eldeen understood about loneliness. It had been hard having Beau overseas. He was gone a total of four years, with one visit home in between. Then she found that in some ways she was lonelier after he returned than before. She thought it was a matter of getting used to one way of life, then having to get used to another one all over again. Cliff offered a cup of coffee, which she declined. The next visit she accepted, and on the third he asked if it were too early in the day for a small whiskey. She didn't think it was. By then Cliff had arranged

his things in a very homey way. The kitchen table had deep
red placemats. The trailing ivy now sat atop the
entertainment center, and reached its way towards the light
from the nearest window. The two wrapped chairs were
gone and replaced with a new sofa. A round coffee table
stood in front covered with neatly laid out magazines whose
titles Eldeen had never seen, *The New Yorker, Atlantic
Monthly, The Economist,* and one she did know, *Arizona
Highways.* Eldeen asked if Cliff had been to Arizona and
he said, yes indeed, several times. He was looking at a little
place out there where he'd go for good, as soon as some of
his investments came due in the fall. Though Eldeen had
only known him for a week or two, she was sad to think
he'd be gone that soon.

Beau's friend, Ty, lifted his beer and took a long swig. The
backs of his hands were spotted with orange, red, blue,
and black. His head, which was shaved, had dots of green.
Beau tried to think how paint had ended up there and didn't
ask. Ty was working on another canvas, a deep swirling thing
that had no beginning and no end. Beau thought it wasn't
so hard to do, throwing paint around like that.

"Old lady with the geezer again?" Ty asked.

"Yup."

Ty burped, leaned back on the sofa, stared at the ceiling
and said, "You should give her a kid."

Beau had had the same thought. A kid would keep
Eldeen at home, where she belonged. This attachment to
the old man was just her needing to take care of someone.
Beau could take of himself, so he wasn't a good substitute.
Women needed to nurture and tend. If he couldn't talk her
into a kid, then he'd suggest a puppy. If she didn't want a
puppy, then she could plant a garden.

"Guy got any money?" asked Ty.

"Who?"

"The geezer."

"Doubt it."

"That's his Cadillac over there, right?"

"So?"

"Looks pretty late-model to me."

Beau finished his beer. He had an urge to throw the bottle at their old television set. "Why the interest in his assets?" he asked.

"Well, if he's as cultured as the old lady says, maybe he'd like to buy one of my paintings."

Having those crazy, loud swirls of color in such a small space would be a lot to take. Beau said he didn't really think so, and got them both another beer.

Finally Beau had to tell Eldeen to stop talking so much about the old man. She was always going on about how interesting he was, and how many places he'd been. Beau said if that were so, then why didn't he take himself off for a long visit somewhere? Eldeen resented that Beau treated Cliff as if he were a nuisance when he was anything but. And it wasn't as if she were neglecting anything there at home. Wasn't his dinner always made and his clothes always washed? Weren't the rugs vacuumed and the dishes always done? And wasn't she bringing in a paycheck, when he wasn't even looking for work? It was the way she was leaning so defiantly on her crutch that made Beau see he had to do something, so he invited her to dinner at Madeleine's.

"Oh, my god, did you get a job?" she asked. She *ka-thumped* her way across their tiny living room and put her arms around him in a three-way hug—her, him, the crutch, which fell to the floor. He accepted her embrace. Her face was shiny and full of light.

"No," he said.

"So, why . . . "

"Can't I do something nice for my own wife once in a

while?" He hadn't meant to sound defensive. She picked up her crutch.

"That's a pricey place. Are you sure it's a good idea?" she asked.

"It's a *great* idea. Now, do you want to go or not?"

"Of course I do, Pumpkin. It'll be awesome."

And it was, until Beau had too much to drink. He was a beer man, unused to hard liquor, and while Eldeen sipped her Bordeaux, Beau downed the whiskey sours. He got giggly, romantic, and surly, all in a row. Then he apologized at length in the truck as Eldeen piloted them through the country darkness. Part of the restaurant's charm was that it was out of the way, in a restored farm house that had once been owned by one of county's wealthiest families. Beau reminded her of this as they drove, then leaned against the window and fell asleep.

Back at the trailer, he snored in his seat. Eldeen couldn't wake him. It was late, she was tired and put out by his behavior that evening, though the food had been awfully good. She'd ordered a beef dish she couldn't pronounce, and found it one of the tastiest things she'd ever eaten. She nudged Beau again with no luck. She thought of poking him hard with the rubber tip of her crutch. She didn't want to leave him there all night in case it got chilly, which it probably wouldn't, but still, it didn't seem right.

The lights were on in Cliff's trailer. Eldeen made her way over, knocked, waited, and then knocked again. Cliff came to the door and said he'd been reading on his chair and must have dropped off. She explained the problem.

"Oh, my dear, what a bother for you! Of course, I'll be right over," Cliff said.

He took a moment to get out of his frayed blue bathrobe and into a pair of jeans and a flannel shirt. The jeans were a surprise. He looked good, she thought, strong and capable. Just the other day he'd mentioned that he still went to the gym three days a week and worked with weights. Eldeen admired him for wanting to stay in shape.

Cliff wrestled Beau out of the truck, leaned him on his shoulder, and walked him to the front door.

"Oops," Beau said. "Oopsie-doopsie."

Cliff guided Beau down the hall to their bedroom, and shoved him onto the bed. Then he lifted his legs off the floor, and got him in the middle, away from the edge.

"Hey, Baby, what say you get naked, get in here, and give your old man a blowjob?" Beau mumbled.

Eldeen's face burned. Cliff pretended he hadn't heard a thing. Back in the living room he said, "Don't be hard on him in the morning. He'll feel rotten enough." Eldeen noticed that she'd stained her dress at the restaurant. It wasn't a new dress, but it was one of her favorites, a little yellow jersey with embroidered roses around the neck. She stepped out of her white sandals, wriggled free of her crutch and sat down. Cliff sat down, too, on the sofa opposite her. The propped up crutch fell loudly to the floor. Cliff reached for it.

"It's okay. Just leave it there," said Eldeen.

"I've been meaning to ask you—"

"Happened when I was six. Fell off a horse I had no business trying to ride. Broke the damn thing so badly, there wasn't a thing anyone could do about it. Not out where we lived, anyway, in the boondocks."

"Oh, I see. I'm sorry. I was going to ask how long you've been married."

Eldeen smiled, and put her hand on her forehead. "Oh, right. Seven years. Why?"

Cliff took a minute to answer. Beau's snores were deep and strong. "Marriage isn't always easy, or intended to always make us happy. It's companionship that counts. As long as you're good companions most of the time."

Eldeen said nothing.

"My wife was a good companion, even when she didn't understand me," said Cliff.

"What didn't she understand?"

"My wanting to feel young again, and explore the world."

"Oh."

"She thought I was—avoiding reality." The shadow of past conversations passed over his face. "So, I practiced. Reality, I mean. That's why I told you right away that I was seventy-two. To get used to how it sounds."

"Are you? Used to it?"

"No."

"Well, you know what they say. 'You're as young as you feel.'" Down the hall Beau turned in bed and mumbled something.

"Can I offer you a nightcap?" Cliff asked.

"Well—" Oh, who cares? she thought. Beau wouldn't wake up until mid-morning, at the earliest.

"That would be lovely," she said. They walked across the road in the silver light of the August moon, and as they climbed the stairs, he patted her shoulder.

Ty watched the barmaid's ass as she wove around the crowded tables. For once his hands were clean. He was in a good mood. He'd actually sold a painting, to a friend of his mother's, which wasn't quite as exciting as selling in a gallery to a stranger, but it was a start. Now he and Beau were celebrating. After the hangover from Madeleine's, Beau had stopped drinking for four days. Today was Friday, and he was ready to pick up where he'd left off.

One of Beau's neighbors, the retired cop, came in with a woman a lot younger than he was. Ty looked up.

"Hey, you know who that chick is? She's a stripper," said Ty.

"No fucking way."

"Way. I saw her at Tattler's once."

"Since when you hang around strip clubs?"

"Always looking for inspiration, you know?"

The retired cop looked at Beau, then leaned over and whispered something in the stripper's ear that made her giggle and bring her hand to her mouth. Maybe he'd seen him the night he came home from Madeleine's, flopped against the old man like a sack of flour, as Eldeen put it. So what if he had? What if Beau had gotten blotto? Mr. Law and Order looked like a guy who did that a lot.

After a couple of minutes Ty asked, "Old lady with her charity again, is she?" Beau nodded. It was really getting to be too much. He'd decided that Eldeen didn't need a kid, but to work in a nursing home so she could play checkers and listen to stupid stories about the good old days. What the hell was wrong with her, anyway?

"She's unhappy," he said. It had come to his mind suddenly and explained everything.

"About what?"

"Don't know."

"That's bad. Unhappy women make unhappy men."

"Where did you get that?"

"I made it up."

"You're full of crap."

"Hey, you tell me I'm wrong."

Ty had a point. Eldeen *had* made him unhappy. And it was all because of Pops over there across the street. Beau would talk to him and suggest that maybe Eldeen shouldn't visit so much, that she needed to be with people her own age. But then he'd just sound like a fool. Eldeen was going to have to come around on her own. With a little encouragement, of course.

"Give me forty bucks," said Beau. "No, better make it fifty."

"What for?"

"Roses. I'm getting Eldeen a dozen red roses."

"Buy them yourself."

"Can't."

"Jesus. I treated you to rounds all afternoon, now you want more from me?"

"It's a loan, that's all."

Ty stared into his beer. Then he reached for his wallet, removed two twenties and a ten.

"Come with me. Help me figure out what to write on the card," said Beau.

"How about, *with love, from your deadbeat hubby.*"

"Fuck off, will you?"

But Ty went along, steered Beau towards pink roses when the red weren't available, saying that yellow or white weren't romantic enough, and told Beau to write *To the love of my life, lovely as these are, your beauty far outweighs.* Beau thought it sounded stupid, but he wrote it anyway, word for word.

Eldeen blushed when she saw the flowers, and her eyes went big and bright, like a kid's. She read the card. Her mouth turned down. She patted Beau's arm, then limped into the bedroom. He heard her crying. He had no idea what to do. How could he comfort her because she was embarrassed at his gift? Where was his *You're so good to me, I never should have neglected you,* and *I promise to do right by you from now on?*

For a few days, Eldeen didn't visit the old man. Then she mentioned that he'd gone out of town.

"Elks convention?" Beau asked.

"Stop it."

"Where, then?"

"He has a friend in Pittsburgh."

"Bet they're painting the town red. Closing the bars. Hitting all the hot spots."

Eldeen's mouth pulled into a narrow line. She sat down, picked up one of his socks that needed mending from a wicker basket she kept by the couch, looked at it, and threw it to the floor.

"What's your problem?" Beau asked. He didn't think it was her period. That had been the week before. Maybe she was coming down with something. Whatever it was, he hoped it wasn't catching.

She closed her eyes for a moment. "I'm sorry. Look, I've been thinking. If you can't find a job, why not take a class at the community college? The recession won't last forever, and in the meantime you can learn something new," she said.

"Like what?"

"I don't know. Computers. Cliff says—"

"I don't give a shit what Cliff says."

Beau went outside to mow the lawn. He'd mowed it only two days ago, but he needed something to do, and it was too early for a beer. He thought about visiting Ty in the garage he used as a studio, but Ty was pretty weird when he was working, so he kept pushing the mower back and forth.

The kids that belonged to the family in the trailer park were running around, playing tag. When they saw Beau sitting on his stairs, they stopped. Their four heads came together in a huddle, then they exploded with laughter and ran away.

Assholes, Beau thought. He was in a lousy mood. Eldeen was out again, he didn't know where. The truck was gone. She hadn't left a note. She used to, all the time, but now she came and went without a word. Beau had no idea what he'd done to make her this way.

A few days later, Eldeen came in from outside, stood in the kitchen, and said she was leaving. She was going to Arizona with Cliff. She and Cliff were in love. She knew Beau thought she was crazy, she knew he didn't understand, that all he saw when he looked at Cliff was an old man. His body might be old, but his spirit was young, and his soul timeless. Those were her exact words. Cliff made her feel what she'd never felt before, that she mattered, that she could belong to someone without feeling owned and all used up. Beau sat on the couch in silence while she went on and on in a calm, even voice, waiting for her to say it was a joke, that she was getting him back for something and wanted to teach him a lesson.

She stopped talking for a minute, maybe to give him a chance to speak. He realized then that she'd been standing the whole time, leaning so hard on her crutch that her knuckles were white.

"You feeding him Viagra or something? I didn't think guys that age could still get it up," said Beau.

"You're disgusting."

"*I'm* disgusting."

Eldeen said that Cliff was better in bed than Beau was. He'd had lots more practice, knew what women needed. Beau's head was in his hands by then. She had another confession to make. She'd been at Cliff's house one afternoon when Beau was out and the neighbor kids must have heard them in the bedroom, because all of a sudden, there they were, with one heaved up on the shoulder of another, giggling and laughing. She realized then that she couldn't go on, sneaking around, that she had to come clean.

"Clean isn't the word I'd use," said Beau. It was dreamlike now. None of this was really happening. She asked him to try to understand, to see that they'd been over since he'd come back from Iraq, that in time he'd be happier without her.

And then she was gone. Her *ka-thump ka-thump* went down the stairs, across the street, followed by the slam of car doors, and the slow acceleration of a very big, very strong motor.

He said her name. He said it again, and remembered the gun. He went to look. She'd left it right there, in the bedside table. He picked it up. There was still time. They had quite a while before they hit the interstate. He moved the gun from one hand to the other and knew it would be easy and right, that he would do it in a second without thinking twice, if only he could figure what to do after that.

THE FALL

S uicides shot up that winter. By Valentine's Day there'd been four. The victims walked out when the light was low, usually in late afternoon, say three or four o'clock. They stood by the rail, *Josh Skinner, age 21, Indianapolis, Indiana,* or *Lisa Finklestein, age 19, Nassau County, New York,* and waited while their classmates went by head-bent against the rising wind, lugging their textbooks home. Lugging their own heavy hearts, too, or so it was generally accepted, given the highly competitive nature of an Ivy League school. Then, when the crowd had thinned or was gone altogether, they jumped into the gorge. Not all went down in waking hours, though. Some crept out in the freezing night. One, *Louis Kennedy, age 22, Santa Barbara, California,* was found in his pajamas. He must have been so miserable, so intent on self-destruction, that even the deep cold couldn't change his mind.

Kirsten's study group lost interest in their Intro. to Econ. class, and focused on the deaths.

"They're like a cult," said Emily. "They need a name. How about The Plungers?"

"That's a plumber's tool," said Lee.

"The Divers, then."

141

They all thought of bronzed cliff divers piercing the surface of a calm, sky-blue sea.

Lee wanted another pitcher of beer, and offered to pay for it himself. Lee's father sent him money whenever he asked for it, which was often. His offer was quickly accepted.

"Look, we better study for the mid-term," said Kirsten.

"We are. We're maximizing our utility," said Tom. His bushy red hair made him seem like someone you couldn't take seriously, Kirsten thought, though he clearly was a serious person.

"Or, we're capturing economies of scale," said Lee. He looked bleary. He wasn't a practiced drinker and wanted to be. He talked about drinking as if it were a sport, something you could win or lose at.

"To stand there, waiting," said Emily. "That's the moment your life changes."

"Bull," said Tom. "The moment your life changes is the moment it ends. The point of impact."

"What about the fall?" asked Lee. "Because then you know it's all over."

"Okay, then, the fall, too. That long, long drop." Tom lifted his hand and sailed it slowly down, back and forth, more like an autumn leaf floating to earth, Kirsten thought, than a body hurtling a hundred feet below.

The beer arrived and was poured out.

"No. It all happens before, when you first consider killing yourself. That's the moment things change," said Emily.

Emily wore nothing but black and pulled her red hair up in a bun so tight the skin by her eyes pulled up, too, giving her an Asiatic look. She had a reckless streak. Sometimes she drank too much and went to bed with the wrong men, yet she kept up her studies, out of deference to her father. She was a good student, better than the rest of them. Kirsten was jealous of her for that. Kirsten struggled to get a B average. She sipped her beer. She didn't like beer, and drank it for the sake of going along.

"Can we change the subject?" asked Lee. Kirsten wished they would. For several nights she had dreamed of falling, but never of hitting earth. In one dream she willed herself not to fall, but to rise, and that was terrifying, too.

"But think about it," said Emily. "Let's say you go to the bridge, you want to jump, you're ready to, then you change your mind."

"And?" asked Lee.

"You go home. It never happened. You didn't jump and you didn't die. No one else would ever know. But you know. You'd always know how close you came. You'd be changed, after that. How could you not be?"

"So, you're saying that wanting to do something and actually doing it are the same thing," said Lee.

"Yes."

"So, our whole lives come down to what we feel, what we desire, whether there's any physical outcome or not."

"Right."

"Wait," said Tom. "Wanting to kill someone isn't the same as actually doing it."

"Or wanting to die and actually dying," added Kirsten.

She pulled her sweaty fingers through her hair. She'd just had it cut in a page boy style that even she had to admit looked like shit. The others had noticed, naturally, but said little. Emily, though, had taken her own hair out of its tight bun and let it drape around her skinny face and shoulders before lifting it once more from her neck. No doubt a way of saying, *I still possess what you gave away!* Before the cut, Kirsten's hair had been long enough to sit on. The change was dramatic, and in the moments before the girl's scissors had closed down, the moment before the first handful had hit the floor, Kirsten, in a panic, forced herself to say nothing and remember that hair, unlike lost lives, will return.

The bar was quiet. Tom, Lee, and Emily occupied their usual booth, fourth from the right by the game room, where two townies were shooting pool and not saying a word to each other.

Kirsten had begged off, down with a cold, Emily said. Tom felt he was closer to her than Emily was, and didn't see why Kirsten hadn't called him to cancel.

"She failed," said Emily.

"What?" asked Lee.

"The midterm. Kirsten failed it. She told me when she called. She said that was another reason not to come today, because she obviously wasn't getting anything out of the group."

"Weird," said Tom. He was worried about her. She'd been growing distant and quiet, even before the exam. When the group began last fall, she would laugh a lot. Tom could see she was nervous and trying not to be. Then she stopped laughing as the end of term approached. After the winter break she came back looking haunted, as if she were listening to something no one else could hear.

Emily shrugged. They drank their beer, opened their textbooks, then closed them again. They'd all aced the same exam Kirsten failed, and it was as if they'd all come to the same conclusion at the same moment—they didn't need to study so hard.

"What's the deal with her hair, anyway?" asked Lee. "Major chop job."

"Looks like she did it herself," said Emily.

"No way. Really?" asked Tom.

"Sure. I can see her standing there, in front of her mirror, going at it with rusty shears."

"Why rusty?"

"Oh, I don't know. There's just something decayed about her."

Tom felt bad again. He didn't like Emily. She was arrogant and cruel, but what she'd said about Kirsten was true.

The Econ. exam was one of three Kirsten failed. She was up to speed in her American History course, but when she opened the exam book to write the essay, she froze. Her mind ran down one path, then up another. Words raced through, and she couldn't capture them, or even slow them down. Geology was a multiple choice, and what tripped her up there was a sudden obsession with filling in the ovals completely—perfectly—with no lead outside the line. The moment she finished one she checked it again and again. She erased several answers to start over from scratch, and when time was called, she'd completed less than half the test. Her failures took air out of whatever room she was in. She went to the health clinic. *I've got asthma,* she told the nurse. A doctor listened hard to her breathing and disagreed. He asked if she were getting enough rest. *Well, you know, we just finished mid-terms.* He said to go and catch up on her sleep.

In her Econ. lecture, she moved to the back, away from Emily, Lee and Tom. Tom turned back sometimes and smiled at her. The others didn't. One day he caught up with her in the hall. She'd tried to escape, and wasn't fast enough.

"Hey," said Tom. "You have time for a beer?" She pulled back, against the wall, and hugged her backpack as if it were a stuffed bear.

"Sure," she said. She'd broken out in a sweat.

"How are things?" asked Tom.

"Fine."

They left the building. Their path took them over the

gorge. Kirsten walked on the outside, away from the railing.
The sunshine was painful. Tom put on a pair of sunglasses.
He looked like a movie star, she thought. Like someone
important.

"We miss you in the study group," he said.

"I bet you don't. At least, Emily and Lee don't."

"Who cares about them? You should come back. If you
think you want to, that is."

"I don't think I'd get much out of it. Besides, I've got a
part-time job now, well, a volunteer job, really, and I won't
be around as much."

"Really? Where are you volunteering?"

"The counseling center."

Kirsten had never been into the counseling center, but
she'd seen a flyer asking for volunteers. *Are you good with
people? Do you have time to listen? No special training necessary.
Call today to attend an orientation session.*

With two beers in her, Kirsten relaxed a little. For some
reason, for the moment she felt safe.

"We should go out some time," said Tom.

"We're out right now."

"I mean at night."

"You mean, like a date?"

"Why not?"

"Okay."

But Tom got busy with school again and didn't ask
Kirsten for a date.

The moment she walked into the counseling center, Kirsten
knew she'd done the right thing. The potted plants were
lush. Tropical. One was red and leafy. Later she realized
they were plastic, and wasn't disappointed. Keeping a
foreign thing like that alive in the Dunston air—even heated
air—would be hard. Yet, when she'd first seen the town,
the spring before, after she'd been admitted, having applied

sight unseen, she found it full of life. Lots of thick green trees and deer off in the roadside woods. Growing up in Los Angeles meant both trees and deer were scarce. She hoped—at times she was dead certain—that coming to school there would mean a much needed renewal. Her own life taking shape, and rounding out.

Her father wanted her to go to Stanford because he had. Though he knew she wanted to escape the house he'd spent his whole life building, and the wife/mother he'd spent years trying to improve, the moment never came when he could admit it to her. *Do us proud* was all he said. Kirsten's mother was devastated. They had never been close, yet she couldn't bear being left alone with a man who thought she was his doormat. The mother knew that her own weakness, her failure to take hold of her own life, had passed on to the daughter, who was equally meek. Yet there was a sliver of steel in her somewhere, her mother was sure. The question was where, and what would cause it to break the surface.

Kirsten was shown to an African-American man who sat at a dusty desk. An ivy plant trailed to the floor. It looked real. Her touch confirmed it. She was confused. The fake plants were in front, and the living ones were in back. Which meant you progressed from death to life, when it was really the other way around. If not, that meant -

"Pray," said the man.

"What?"

"Name's Pray." He pointed to a piece of wood on his desk.

"Odd name."

"Even before I was born, my mother was convinced my soul needed saving."

"Did it?"

"I've been pretty good so far, but it's too soon to tell."

His teeth were very white. The dreadlocks she wasn't sure about. She'd always thought they looked stupid.

"So, what can I do for you?" he asked.

"I'd like to volunteer."

"That's great. Why would you like to volunteer here, as opposed to say, an animal shelter?"

Was he baiting her?

"Because people seem to be in trouble," she said. "The stress seems to be building up."

"That's probably true. Well, Kirsten, why don't you tell me a little bit about yourself?"

It was like talking about someone else. Growing up in Brentwood, coming to the Ivy League to study—what, she wasn't sure. Maybe theater, though she was terrified of performing; so maybe history, though the relevance of that wasn't always clear because all of us, even historians, had to live in the moment, didn't they; so maybe Economics, since that seemed to be what made the world go around—the trouble was she'd just failed her exam, and the grade report had already been sent home, and she could just imagine how it would be received. Her father could ooze disappointment like pus from a wound (she then apologized for her choice of words).

She talked more. It got easier. There were so many random points in her life, all these things off the side, like how her aunt tried to show her how to paint once and got fed up with her, or how she'd fallen in love with a palomino pony her father said was too much responsibility for her, or how her piano teacher once told her she was probably wasting her time. She told Pray she thought she was supposed to connect all the points somehow, like the picture puzzles kids used to do, because she was sure there was something underneath all the dots, if she could only get far enough away to really look down and see it.

Pray told her she should make an appointment with one of the counselors there. She thought he meant so she could learn what to tell people who came in, at the end of their rope.

"It never hurts to explore these feelings in a safe environment," he said.

The moment she realized he thought she was nuts, she stood up and left.

The snow came on hard. A March snow was supposed to have less force, or so she'd been told. Or had she ever been told what snow was supposed to do, and if so, when? Kirsten's room-mate spent all her time at her boyfriend's frat, leaving Kirsten on her own. It was better that way. Celia, the roommate, talked a lot and wore perfume that made Kirsten's throat itch. The moment she left, taking the scent with her, Kirsten stopped coughing.

The snow fell for two days and three nights, and on the morning of the third day the world had become visible once more, and blindingly bright. All the sunlight in Southern California was nothing compared to this, yet Kirsten didn't mind squinting her way across the main quad, across the gorge where icicles hung like huge teeth, around the athletic center, past the Physics building, along the edge of College Town, then back to her dorm. She hadn't attended any of her classes for ten days. When that time reached a total of two weeks, a letter would be mailed home, or so the student hand-book had said. Her father had suffered the grade report in silence, but she was sure the letter would prompt a telephone call, or worse, his appearance at her door. But no, he wouldn't waste his time coming all that way to fetch her back. He'd tell her to get on the next plane home. He'd make himself scarce when she did return, avoiding conversation, avoiding her, avoiding, avoiding, avoiding. Her mother wouldn't meet her eye, and then one morning, Kirsten would awaken to find her sitting on the end of her bed, watching her sleep.

She couldn't go home. Not after submitting herself so easily to failure. She'd have to stay right there in Dunston, and suffer it out, moment by moment.

Her room felt too small, even with Celia gone. She moved Celia's dresser into the hall, wrestled her desk out there, too, and stripped her bed. The R.A. asked what she was doing. Kirsten explained.

"You can't do that. This room is assigned as a double. Everything has to go back the way it was."

Kirsten promised to replace the furniture. She locked the door. The room still felt small. She tore down the curtains, and hoped the light would widen everything it fell on. It didn't. She needed a shower. She hadn't had one for four days. The sight of her own nakedness had become disturbing. There were too many mirrors in the bathroom. She thought they should be painted black to spare her having to see herself. She gathered what she needed—shampoo, soap, a towel that stank of mildew because she'd never once put it through the laundry, different clothes, none of them clean—and made her way into the bathroom. She turned off the light. Without windows, she stood in total darkness. This is what the blind experience all the time. That was both fascinating and terrifying. She inched towards the shower stall, put her things just outside it on the floor, and slid her hand along the cold, smooth tile until she found the lever that turned on the water. She stripped. She found her soap and shampoo, and got into the stall. As she was rinsing her hair, the light went on.

"What the fuck are you doing taking a shower in the dark?" The voice belonged to a fat girl two doors down. Kirsten had never learned her name. She didn't answer.

"Oh, and you might want to close the curtain."

Kirsten saw that she'd soaked the clothes she'd intended to wear because there'd been nothing to block the water.

She pushed down the lever, wrapped herself in her wet towel, gathered her belongings, then returned to her room and wept.

Tom knocked on her door. He smelled of fresh air and the Indian food he'd had for lunch. His presence made the room warm.

"You look like shit, if you don't mind my saying so," he said. His backpack hit the floor.

"I'm fine."

"Have you been sick?"

"No. Just working hard."

"You haven't been in class."

"I needed some time off."

He sat down on the end of her bed. She'd been sleeping in a sleeping bag on the floor. When she heard the knock, she'd kicked the bag under the bed.

"You look like you could use some fresh air," he said. "Let's go for a walk."

"It's freezing."

"It'll do you good."

They sat, not talking for a while. As he was leaving, he hugged her. She didn't understand why. She felt his heart beat through his tee shirt, and flannel shirt, and the sweater he wore over all of that, and the heavy coat on the outside. How could that be? How could anyone's heart be that strong?

The moment the door closed behind him, the room rushed outwards, spreading like a stain. That's stupid, she thought. It's just a room.

The hour was late. She'd been up all night for the second day straight. She was hungry. A candy bar from the vending machine downstairs would really hit the spot, and then the thought turned her stomach. Tom had called twice. She hadn't answered. If she saw him, she'd say her phone had run down. *Out of juice*, she'd say. *Like a squeezed orange.*

Then the moment came when she could no longer stand the confines of her room. She dressed in layers. Ice crystals lay on the black window, brightened here and there by the street lamp three floors below. Outside, the paths were black and the snow was white, but a dim white, as if the life and power had been drained from it.

Snow that lay in darkness must have a name, she thought. Night snow? But its color. What was the color, exactly? Were colors exact or approximate? Was this something she was supposed to know? Did anyone know?

Too many questions, and not enough answers. That was her problem. How could she go through life in this state of constant ignorance? Is that why people ended it, because there were too many things they didn't know? Or, was it knowing that they'd never find out? And seeing that death was the one big mystery, the one thing no one really knew for sure, they hastened it, rushed into it, all for that desperate need to know.

Her boots were silent as they hit the ground. No one was out. The world had gone completely still. The only thing moving was the silver plume of her own breath. She heard the water in the gorge well before she reached the bridge. The sound was like a song of defiance, because the water was stronger than the cold. The water did not freeze.

She felt nothing. Not the bitter air. Not fear. Not regret. She'd stopped thinking about the people she'd once known, how they would take her end, what their lives would be like as they moved forward without her.

The railing was under construction. Renovation, actually. A guard was being placed that would prevent climbers from being able to jump unless they snuck by at either end. She stood there, aware of the challenge, but also of a change in the light around her. It was growing brighter. Dawn was underway. She'd never been awake at dawn before, never seen the sun rise. The first and last, she thought, then felt the idea was trite.

Then the light rose enough so that an icicle hanging from a dark ledge of shale was illuminated. It seemed to glow. Kirsten had never seen anything so beautiful. She didn't understand how the light had reached the ice before falling on anything else. Soon other icicles were coming to life, turning a faint, warm yellow.

"My god," she said, holding the rail with her gloved hands.

"Are you all right?" a man's voice asked. She turned. All there was of him was his thick coat and wool hat. He asked the question again.

"Look at the gorge. Look at the light. Isn't it amazing?"

The man turned. He didn't seem to know what she was talking about.

"It's damn early to be up and about," he said.

"It's beautiful."

"I work on campus. I have to be there by six. That's why I'm out here, freezing my ass off."

She said nothing.

"What are you doing out here, if you don't mind my asking?" he asked.

Suddenly, she no longer knew. She was cold. And tired, and very hungry. She continued to look at the icicles and realized the man wasn't going to walk off until she went, too. She gazed down, hearing the water rush, held by the dawn, feeling as if she herself were lit from within.

Our Love Could
Light the World

The old lady had died some time that spring. No one knew exactly when, because she'd been shut up in a nursing home forever, and then one day the son came around with a mover and that was that. The whole place was cleaned out. Minor repairs were done to the outside. As to the inside, it was hard to say for sure. People up and down the street who'd been there long enough to remember the old lady remembered a cramped, ugly kitchen, with Formica counter tops and a vinyl dinette set. While she was gone no one had lived there. The son came by every now and then and made sure things were okay, and people wondered why he didn't just take charge and sell the place. It wasn't as if she'd ever come back, the old lady. Once you went into a nursing home that's where you stayed. Until the funeral parlor, and that little plot of ground you hoped someone had been good enough to buy for you in advance.

Then the Dugans moved in. Although the street wasn't particularly close-knit—no block parties or pleasant pot-lucks—the neighbors welcomed them. Their efforts were ignored. The Dugans had moved seven times in the last ten years, and the idea of putting down roots was just plain silly. Soon, the neighbors made comments. Not only were the Dugans unfriendly, they were noisy and didn't collect the shit their dog left wherever it wanted, usually in someone else's yard.

Mrs. Dugan left every morning at exactly seven-thirty. She got into her car, a rusty green Subaru, wearing a suit. Her hair was up in a bun. She even carried a briefcase. No one knew what she did. One man said she worked in a bank. The woman across from him said she sold insurance.

Mr. Dugan didn't work because he'd hurt his back years before on a construction site. The disks he'd ruptured eventually went back in place, but not before causing permanent scarring and calcium deposits which caused pain that ranged from annoying to agonizing. He was never without pain, in fact, and had a standing prescription for Vicadin which mixed badly with alcohol. That's why he was reduced to drinking only beer, instead of his beloved whiskey. You had to give your body the space it needed, he told his kids. No two ways about that.

Five children made up the family. The eldest was Angelica, a fat, teenage girl with a nose ring and short, spiky green hair. She ruled her siblings with a steady stream of insults. Her favorites were "dumbass," "dumbshit," and "horsedick."

The next in line was Timothy. The cast in his left eye was a painless affliction. He wasn't aware of it until people stared hard, then looked away in embarrassment. A baby-sitter once told him it was a gift from God, proof that Timothy was special. The baby-sitter was an old woman whose saggy chin sported a forest of short, white hairs.

Twin girls, Marta and Maggie, came just after Timothy. Mr. Dugan had objected to the German name, Marta. He thought the German people were fat, pretentious slobs. Far too young to ever have been directly involved in the Second World War, his sentiment stemmed from a boss he once had, Otto Klempt, who told Mr. Dugan he was the laziest worker he'd ever had in his storeroom. Oddly enough, Marta was rather like Mr. Klempt in temperament, harsh and scornful. Maggie was quiet on the surface, yet full of deep longings and desires she was afraid to share. One day, she was sure, she'd be on the stage, and very, very rich. Her husband would do everything for her—in her later years she'd see that she developed this idea from watching her mother bully her father—and she'd take every gesture with the same mysterious smile she gave her other fans.

The youngest was Foster. The name was based on a statement Mrs. Dugan made, that if she had any more children they'd end up in foster care. Foster had been born with a twisted leg that gave him a definite hitch in his stride, but otherwise did little to slow him down. He was a pleasant child, despite the generally sullen atmosphere of his household.

All in all, the five children didn't particularly care for one another, and they didn't dislike each other, either. One thing they knew was that they stood as a pack against the rest of the world, a term that had special significance after one of their neighbors came home to find them all roller skating in his driveway, where they'd apparently knocked over his trash cans in the process, and called them a pack of wild dogs.

He was punished for that. Paper bags full of dog shit, carefully collected over the week from their mutt, Thaddeus, were set afire seconds before a frantic knock on the door, made by Maggie, their fastest. Answering the call, the neighbor found the growing blaze and reacted as anyone would, by stamping it out. HAHAHAHAHA, the children thought to themselves, individually, in the privacy of their own thoughts, for that caper, like all their others, was born in committee, yet appreciated alone.

Angelica felt the lack of community most. *We don't have*

enough family time, is what she concluded. She'd seen families spend time together. Across the street, the Morrises were always having cook-outs, and batting balls, and playing badminton. The children—two, maybe three—laughed a lot. The mother never yelled, and the father had a strong, steady gait. She knew her own family could never be like that, yet she wished they could.

Mrs. Dugan came home from work tired. She was often crabby, too. She worked in the sales department for a small company that sold manufactured homes. Her job was to walk clients through their purchase options. The people she dealt with had all fallen on hard times, or were old and looking to down-size. None had the flush of optimism. Mrs. Dugan thought she herself had once been full of hope and ambition which, over time, had been whittled away. She decided to give herself a kick in the pants, and when the chance came to represent the company at a regional conference, she put in her bid, and even took her boss out for lunch.

She was chosen. She walked on air. Mr. Dugan didn't like the idea of her spending three days down in Wilkes-Barre. He was glum, and snuck sips of whiskey from a flash he kept on a shelf in his closet.

"Three days, Potter. One, two, three," said Mrs. Dugan. She couldn't wait. She loved her family, and she hated them, too, and lately the balance had been tipping towards hate.

"And just what is it you plan to do at this conference?" Mr. Dugan looked like he was about to put his head through a brick wall, something Mrs. Dugan used to admire about him and now found exhausting.

"Attend presentations. Walk around the convention floor. See what other vendors are doing to improve sales."

"Sounds boring."

"Only a boring person would say that."

The stone face melted. His mouth turned down.

"I'm sorry, Potter. I didn't mean that. You're not boring."

"Yes I am, or you wouldn't have said it."

He took himself off to the small back room he called his den and lay down on the couch. He watched the dust dance in the light. Maybe three days wouldn't be so bad. Three days wasn't all that long. He could get a lot of good drinking done in three days. The thought cheered him.

Over dinner, Mrs. Dugan laid out the program.

"Angelica, you're in charge. But you don't do all the work—share it equally. Start getting ready for school. There's only another week left. When you're not doing that, I want you each to clean your rooms. When you're done with that, take turns weeding the garden." The neighbors complained most about the garden. "And make sure Thaddeus gets his walks regular. I don't want to come home to a house full of dog poop."

Around the table the faces were still. The children had never been away from their mother before. Plans of mischief were being born, right there, as forks were lifted to mouths, and pieces of inedible pot roast were slipped unseen to Thaddeus below the table. Angelica knew where her mother kept some extra money. That would come in handy when she took off for the mall. The twins planned to stay up all night watching TV. Timothy and Foster would live on ice cream and candy. They'd been handed a vacation, and they intended to make the most of it.

Mrs. Dugan packed her bag in a state of excitement and fear. She didn't have very nice clothes, although they were respectable. Which of her four blouses would go best with the brown suit? Where she'd never given much thought before to her appearance at work, she was now overcome with self-criticism and doubt. She had to look the part. She was an executive on the move. Secretly she yearned for a promotion, more money, and to get the family out of rental homes and into a place of their own. That thought made her sit down suddenly on her bed. The promotion might come, as might the money and home ownership, but the people who lived there would be the same—lazy, unkempt, and bad-tempered.

"Change your mind?" Mr. Dugan asked when he found her there some time later, still sitting. Some strands of her naturally blonde hair had escaped her bun and floated around her small, pretty face.

"No. Just taking a break." And with that she was up, finished packing, put her bag by the front door so she wouldn't forget it in the morning, then shouted for her children to get ready for bed.

The sunlight that first day—Tuesday—said it would be hot. The house was not air conditioned. If they were lucky, the children could get their father to drive them out to the lake and swim. They liked going to the lake. One look at him passed out in the den put an end to that particular plan. Angelica said they should give Thaddeus a bath. The others agreed. A small, dirty plastic wading pool was put to use. Thaddeus didn't think any of it was a good idea, and bolted from the tub the moment soap was applied and his fur scrubbed. He escaped the yard in no time, an easy feat since there was no fence, and bounded across the street where Mrs. Hooper was trimming her rose bush. Thaddeus stopped right in front of her and shook, sending water and suds everywhere. Mrs. Hooper shrieked and called the dog an ugly name, called the children watching from their porch an even uglier name, and then threatened to call the police when Angelica turned around, bent over, and dropped her pants. No one came to fetch Thaddeus. Everyone knew from experience that he'd return eventually, which he did, the moment a can of dog food was opened in the kitchen.

After Thaddeus enjoyed his lunch and dropped soapy water on the floor, boredom returned. Foster applied a

Band-Aid to each of his eyes—top to bottom—and groped his way through the living room where Timothy was on the floor coloring.

"What the fuck's wrong with you?" Angelica asked. She was sitting in their mother's stained easy chair, flipping through an old magazine.

"Want to know what it's like being blind." Foster tripped over someone's jacket, collected himself, and continued, arms outstretched.

Maggie passed him in her ballet shoes. She was practicing standing on her toes. It hurt a lot. She thought of hovering over the dusty wood-planked stage to the silent, tense awe of the audience.

"Watch out, dumbass!" Angelica said when Maggie lurched across Timothy. "Jesus, what's wrong with everyone today?"

Pizza was ordered for dinner. After all dimes, nickels, and stray pennies were gathered from every pocket, drawer, stray sock. Mr. Dugan grieved. "Where the hell's my wallet?" When he couldn't find it he sat at the kitchen table and stared into space. The children recognized this mood. Their mother was both the cause and cure. She'd called to say she'd gotten there safely. Timothy had answered the phone. There was noise in the background, a man's voice, the sound of tinny music. Mr. Dugan took the receiver and told everyone to leave him alone so he could have a civilized conversation, for once, which he did for about forty-five seconds before Mrs. Dugan hung up.

At noon the following day, Angelica went to dress and had no clean underwear. Foster lacked a clean shirt, and Mr. Dugan's sock drawer was empty. Monday was laundry day, and Monday was the day Mrs. Dugan had packed her bag. She hadn't done the laundry. Her oversight was painful to Mr. Dugan, because it strengthened his suspicion that his wife was essentially dissatisfied with her life. He called the children into the kitchen and told them to start washing clothes. Maggie took charge and trotted down the basement stairs. She returned to report that there was no more laundry detergent. A debate ensued. Could dish soap be used? What about shampoo? Angelica told everyone to shut up, ordered her father to find his damn wallet, give her some money, and wait until she returned from the store.

"Let me go, let me!" Foster was hopping up and down. The store was a ten-minute walk, yet Angelica doubted Foster's ability to successfully choose and pay for a bottle of detergent on his own. Foster was only eight. She told Timothy and the twins to go with him. Safety in numbers, she figured. With four of them, not much could go wrong.

She jotted down some other necessary items on a list. Milk, bread, eggs, frozen fish sticks, ice cream, chewing gum, and mayonnaise.

"I want a candy bar," said Marta.

"Me, too," said Timothy.

"You get this stuff, first. If there's money left over, fine."

The children left. Angelica put the dirty dishes in the sink. The sink was full, so placing them was tricky. She passed by her father's den.

"Angie! Hey, Angie! There's a guy on TV eating goldfish! What do you think about that?" he called out.

"That's pretty neat, Dad."

In her room—which was hers alone after a bitter fight with Mrs. Dugan about who would sleep where—she applied black nail polish with great care. She loved painting her nails. She loved painting other people's nails. She once painted all the nails of her siblings—including the boys'—a fiery red. The effect was stunning. Mrs. Dugan called her an idiot, and demanded that it be removed at once. Mrs. Dugan had lost her sense of humor, Angelica realized. There was a time when her mother laughed, danced about in her bedroom slippers, and bestowed gentle affection on her family.

Next, she checked her cell phone. It was a cheap phone, gotten at great personal cost of begging and wheedling. Mrs. Dugan had been unmoved by Angelica's repeated statement that all the kids at school had cell phones. In the end, a cheap, poorly made cell phone with chronically bad reception found its way into Angelica's loving hands. She liked to send text messages on it. There was one boy she sent messages to. The boy, Dwayne, had been in her math class the year before and she thought he was fabulous. She hungered for Dwayne the way she hungered for mint chocolate-chip ice cream. The messages she sent were bland, non-committal things like, *TV sucks today. What's up?* His replies were equally bland: *Nothing,* and *baseball practice,* and *cleaning out garage.* Yet into each she read a special meaning, a deeper truth that when added up in time would prove that he felt for her what she felt for him. There was no message from Dwayne. He hadn't texted her for two whole days, and her nerves were about to snap.

She texted her sometime best friend, Luann. *no mssg. from D. means what?* Luann texted back, *phone's probably off. or battery ran down.* Luann's brutal logic was painful, not comforting at all. If Dwayne cared so little about staying in touch that he turned off his phone, or let the battery die, then what Angelica feared—that this relationship was completely one-sided—was true.

She shoved the phone in her pocket and went downstairs. The house was quiet. Her father had switched to a game show, and the sound of clapping and cheers was like a party from another planet. *Planet Party,* she thought, and wanted to write that down. Every now and then she made notes of random thoughts thinking that they, like the messages from Dwayne, would one day contain a brilliant and tragic truth about the human condition that only she was sensitive enough to see and appreciate.

The children hadn't returned from the store. The clock

said they'd been gone almost an hour. She was furious at
the idea that she might have to go looking for them.

"Boneheads," she said, and ate a slice of cold pizza left
over from the night before.

Twenty minutes later, Angelica saw the four children
walking slowly up the street. Foster was in the lead. Behind
him, Timothy carried a single bag of groceries. The twins
followed, with an old man in between them. Each girl held
one of the old man's hands. The old man was shuffling
along, bobbing his head. His white hair was bright in the
sun. He wore a plaid bathrobe over blue pajamas, and
bedroom slippers.

"Jesus Christ," she said. She looked in on her father. He
was asleep on the couch. The television set was on and a
muscular young woman in work-out garb was jogging on a
treadmill with a forced smile on her sweaty face. Angelica
felt what she always did when she saw a body like that—
deep, agonizing envy. She was thirty pounds overweight,
and the last time she'd been to the doctor she'd been warned
of the dangers of developing diabetes, which more and more
young fat people were.

The children came through the back door with the old
man in tow.

"Who the fuck is this?" Angelica asked.

"We found him," Timothy explained.

"Found him? Where?"

"At the store," said Marta.

"Outside the store. On a bench, in the shade," said
Maggie.

"Can we keep him? I think we should keep him," said
Foster.

They put the old man in a chair at the kitchen table.
His blue eyes were watery and empty.

"Caroline," he said, when he saw Angelica.

The old man smelled of camphor.

"Why the hell did you bring him here?" Angelica asked.

"We told you. He was on a bench. No one came out to get him, so we figured he was lost."

"Sir, what's your name?" Angelica asked and peered hard at the old man.

"Caroline," he said.

"Great. Did you check his wallet?"

"Doesn't have one," said Timothy. Timothy was the most resourceful of them all.

"He gave me a lollipop. There are more, if you want one," said Foster.

Sure enough, the old man had three lollipops in the pocket of his bathrobe.

Maggie put the groceries away. Angelica saw that they'd forgotten the laundry detergent and the mayonnaise. And the eggs. She sat down. The day had become difficult.

"Well, he obviously wandered away from somewhere, so someone must be looking for him," said Angelica.

"They won't find him. We'll hide him, and then say he's our grandfather, or something," said Foster.

"Are you out of your fucking mind? Where's he going to sleep?" Angelica asked.

"With us. He can have the top bunk, and we'll share the bottom one," said Maggie.

"He might fall out of the top bunk. Better put him down below," said Marta.

"Caroline," said the old man.

"Sir, who is Caroline?" Angelica asked.

The old man smiled. His teeth were perfectly white and strong.

"Is Caroline your wife? Is Caroline looking for you? Can we call Caroline?" Angelica asked.

The old man looked at her vacantly. She might as well have been speaking Greek. She had to do something, but she had no idea what. The old man whimpered. He sounded like a puppy looking for its mother's milk. Angelica ordered the twins to open and heat a can of soup. They argued about whether split pea or tomato was best. They settled on tomato. Foster tied a dish towel around the old man's neck. They put the bowl of soup in front of him. The old man looked at it, and whimpered.

"Help him, then. Jesus," said Angelica.

Timothy lifted a spoonful of soup. The old man opened his mouth like a toddler would. He took the soup, swallowed, and opened his mouth again. He consumed the entire bowl.

"Maybe he ran away because he was hungry," Foster said.

"He didn't run away, stupid. He wandered off. Someone didn't lock the door," said Angelica. Then she realized that a search might be underway, and bulletins issued about the old man being missing. She went into her father's den and turned to the news. A tanker truck had exploded on an overpass in Indiana. A hurricane was speeding towards the coast of North Carolina. The President gave a speech about the economy to a crowd of angry, sullen-looking people. Closer to home the local teacher's union had rejected the latest contract proposal. No one was looking for the old man.

Mr. Dugan opened his eyes. "What's up? I thought I heard voices," he said.

"Nothing. Go back to sleep."

"I'm ready for some lunch."

"I'll bring it to you in here."

"That's okay. I need a little stretch."

"Dad, don't."

"What? Stretch?"

Angelica explained about the old man. Mr. Dugan sat up and stared at the worn rug at his feet. He nodded. He cleared his throat.

"You did the right thing," he said.

They both went into the kitchen. The old man's head had drooped down towards his chest. He snored loudly. Mr. Dugan said that if there were any soup left, he'd appreciate a nice bowl with a slice of buttered bread. Thaddeus stood by the old man's side, sniffing his leg. The other children were all seated at the table, each in his usual chair. The chair they'd put the old man in was Mrs. Dugan's. Angelica prepared her father's lunch. Her cell phone buzzed in her pocket. Luann had asked, *anything?* Angelica quickly wrote back, *no!*

"I think we should vote," said Foster.

"On what?" asked Maggie.

"On whether or not we're going to keep him."

"We can't keep him. He's not ours," said Mr. Dugan. "I'll call the police after lunch. They'll handle it."

"No! Daddy don't do that. Please!"

"Now, listen. This is a person, not a pet. Even if he were a pet, we'd have to find out if he belonged to someone else. In the case of a person, you can be well-assured that he does, in fact, belong to someone else."

Mr. Dugan was proud of his speech. He was very sorry his wife wasn't there to hear it. The old man went on snoring. The twins got up from the table.

"Oh, well," said Marta. "Too bad." They went into their room. The boys stayed behind. Mr. Dugan called the police. His voice was bright and polished. He seemed happy. Angelica wasn't happy. She was gripped by a growing sense of alarm.

"Someone will be along in a while," said Mr. Dugan.

"Do they know who he is?" asked Angelica.

"No. They said it happens all the time. The nursing home might not even know he's gone, yet."

"Assholes."

"Exactly."

The old man lifted his head and stared around him. He blinked. Mr. Dugan helped him from his chair, and guided him into the living room.

"Come on, Pops. You'll be more comfortable in here. There you go. Want your feet up? No? Okay. Just sit there, and stay out of trouble."

Angelica sat down next to him. The old man fussed. He plucked at the belt of his bathrobe and moaned.

"What's wrong with him?" asked Angelica. She's was afraid he was sick, or about to die. That wouldn't be good, if he just up and died on them. Mr. Dugan left and returned quickly with glass of amber liquid.

"Maybe he needs a little nip," said Mr. Dugan.

"What if he's on medication?" asked Angelica.

"Won't hurt him." Mr. Dugan brought the glass to the old man's lips. The old man tasted the liquid. His eyes squinted and a gurgle rose from his throat. Mr. Dugan gave a thumb's up. The old man nodded. He gave the old man another swallow. Timothy and Foster wandered into the living room. They were bored, now. The old man didn't interest them anymore. Timothy picked up his coloring from yesterday, and Foster considered putting another set of Band-Aids on his eyes, then decided to wrap Thaddeus's toes together with masking tape. He'd done that before, and Thaddeus didn't seem to mind at all.

The old man held Angelica's hand. His skin was very smooth, as if it hadn't touched anything rough in years and years. How long had he been like that? What, if anything, did he remember of his past?

"Well, I'm going back to my den for a little while, so you just sit here with him," said Mr. Dugan

"What if he needs to go to the bathroom?" asked Angelica.

"You better hope he doesn't."

The old man had settled down. He fell asleep once more. Angelica's phone buzzed. It was Luann.

going to the mall. want to come?

The old man's grip was surprisingly tight, so Angelica had to type with only one hand.

can't.

why?

grandpa's here.

oh. text me later.

k.

Timothy got tired of coloring, and went up to his room. Foster doodled on the back of an unopened bill. Thaddeus padded by, slightly impaired by the tape. Gradually, Angelica relaxed. She wondered what Dwayne was doing. She could text him and say, *guess whose hand I'm holding right now?* Then she wouldn't explain, and look sly when she saw him at school. That might shake him up. Dwayne needed shaking up. Dwayne was too laid back. She wondered what the old man was like when he was younger. Maybe he was as dull as toast until Caroline came along. Then Caroline turned his head. Caroline made him change his mind about everything. He went on breathing in a deep, steady rhythm. He might live quite a few more years, Angelica thought. If he was well cared for, that is. Looking after an old man like that wouldn't be so hard, except for the bathroom issue. It occurred to her that wiping someone's ass might not be the easiest thing in the world.

The old man stirred, opened his eyes, and focused them hard on Angelica. He smiled. He leaned towards her, and planted a dry kiss on her lips. In a thin, wobbly voice he said, "Our love could light the world."

Eventually the police arrived and escorted the old man out. Angelica held his hand until the very last minute. He was a resident of the Clearview nursing home, only a half-mile away. An employee of the nursing home had come in a separate car and told Angelica about the service she'd performed that day, and how heart-warming it was to see a young person be so caring and responsible. Mr. Dugan emerged from his den and stood with Angelica and the other children on the front porch and waved good-bye. Angelica went to sit on her bed and think. Her mother would be home the day after tomorrow, and school would start the week after that. Time seemed like a slow, lazy river they were all floating along. Only the river in the old man's heart had flowed backwards, returning him to Caroline, whoever she was. To love someone so much that you'd never forget her, even when you'd forgotten everything else. That was something. That was worth having. As she checked her phone again to see if Dwayne had texted her, already knowing that he hadn't, she decided that one day, no matter what, she would.

ANNE LEIGH PARRISH's short stories have appeared or are forthcoming in *The Virginia Quarterly Review, Clackamas Literary Review, The Pinch, American Short Fiction, PANK, Knee-Jerk Magazine, Prime Number Magazine, C4, Eclectica Magazine, Storyglossia, Bluestem,* and *r.kv.r.y.,* among other publications. Her awards include *The Pinch* 2008 Literary Award in Fiction for "Surrogate"; First Place in the *American Short Fiction* 2007 Short Story Contest for "All The Roads That Lead From Home"; and First Place in the 2003 Clark College Fiction Contest for "Fance."

For more information about Anne and her work, visit her website at www.anneleighparrish.com.

Cover artist **LYDIA SELK** lives in Washington State with her husband. He gave her a digital camera about six years ago. That gift ignited a passion. She tries to capture tiny stories whispered from abandoned and decaying objects, from trees in the forest, or from the back alleys in her hometown. See her work at www.flickr.com/photos/lydiafairy.

CPSIA information can be obtained at www.ICGtesting.com
Printed in the USA
BVOW011409180911

271445BV00001B/3/P